Falsetto in the Woods

HAUNTED REQUIEMS

Falsetto in the Woods

A NOCTURNE SYMPHONY NOVELLA

4 Horsemen
Publications, Inc.

LYRA R. SAENZ

4 Horsemen Publications, Inc.
1497 Main St. Suite 169
Dunedin, FL 34698
4horsemenpublications.com
info@4horsemenpublications.com

Typeset by Michelle Cline
Edited by JM Paquette

Library of Congress Control Number: 2021944768

Print ISBN: 978-1-64450-337-9
Audio ISBN: 978-1-64450-335-5
Ebook ISBN: 978-1-64450-336-2

Table of Contents

Dedication

To my loving partner who puts up with my love for everything horror despite having no inclination toward the genre personally. My love, you always take the time to buy me the latest Stephen King novel and discuss with me all of the reasons why something does or does not work in whatever I'm currently binging. Thank you for your love of physics and logic. You've made my writing stronger.

And...

To all the girls whose favorite color is black, to my spook–lovers who can't wait for fall, and to the spirits of those who have come and gone before me,

Happy Halloween!

A Walk in the Black Forest

Hexennacht Eve – 30th Day in the Month of Darkness – 1870 A.P.

S HE DRUMS HER NAILS AGAINST THE DASH-board. Hanging from the rearview mirror, the pine-apple air freshener swings violently back and forth, back and forth as Sebastian's truck bounces over the cracks and bumps in the beatendown dirt road. The glass of the window is cool against her forehead, a distraction from the motion sickness bubbling in her stomach. Every time she opens her eyes it gets worse, but closing them isn't much better. The world spins, rapidly descending spirals that make her feel like she's being flushed down a toilet.

"We're almost there, babe," says Sebastian, her boyfriend of two years, reaching over to thread his fingers through her hair. He presses his thumb into the pressure point just under one of the tech nodes at her temple. The metal plate under-neath her skin throbs in response, a wave of relief washing through her synapses.

She sighs. She doesn't normally get motion sickness this badly, but her internal network has been on the fritz since the last dead zone they drove through, and she doesn't need to check her comm to know they're completely off grid.

"I cannot believe I let you convince me to go on a stupid camping trip."

"Oh, come on, city girl. Give it a chance. It'll be fun. You told me you've never been outside of a training exercise." The wheels bolt over another uneven ridge, tossing the car wildly enough Lily's stomach jolts into her throat.

"Couldn't we have just gone to a theme park? There are plenty of haunted houses at Kosmos World. Surely, there's a ghost–themed one this year."

And this drive is getting right up there with some of the milder roller coasters.

"*Fake* ghosts. People wearing make–up, fake blood, and plastic teeth. If it weren't for the dark lighting, they wouldn't be scary at all."

"The holoprojections are pretty realistic."

"We went to Fright Fest last year, Lil." He cranks the stick shift into park. "Besides, my brother's been scouting this place out for his next ghost tour. We'll be his first critics before he opens officially."

Now that they've stopped, her insides cease their acrobatics, and she opens her eyes to look at him, dressed in his driving leathers, plaid shirt, and blue jeans. His sun–kissed hair flops airily around his cheekbones, sunny golden bangs, ruffled from the knit beanie on his head and hanging in loose curls over his sunglasses. She envies his tan, still a bronzy honeycomb despite prime swimming season having long since passed. The evidence of what little bit of sun she managed to get has already disappeared, not that it did more than darken her freckles and dry out her strawberry blonde hair, leaving it in frizzly strings around her head.

Thank the gears for moisturizing shampoo!

"Here I thought your idea of Halloween fun was entertaining trick–or–treaters with your horrid Count Dracula accent and wearing those fake fangs that give you the most horrible slur."

He makes an affronted face at her, dimples showing through the scruff of his facial hair, the warm browns of his eyes bright in the setting sun.

"I'll show you 'horrible'!" He digs his fingers into her sides, eliciting a shrieking laugh out of her. She swats the rogue digits away, delivering two smacks to his chest for good measure. He laughs her off and gestures to the landscape past the frost–edged windows like an auction house conductor. "But babe, look at this! Can you honestly tell me this isn't one of the most beautiful sights you've ever seen?"

Lily draws herself out of the door to look, and oh, he's right. He is very right.

Beyond the portals of their humble vehicle, a boundless forest stretches, lush with orange, yellow, and red leaves. The colors are as breathtaking as the sunset, like the whole forest has gone up in flames—the kind of place that would inspire painters and musicians to create masterpieces.

Nothing like the piteous groves in New London. Their inner–city home is too far south to see true seasonal changes and too urbanized to hold a candle to this majesty. Even the largest city park, Abney Gardens—hailed as one of the most visited tourist spots in all of Aighneas—has hardly any trees in it. Well... any real trees anyway. Plenty of synthetics, hybrids bred to thrive on city pollution and clean the smog out of the air. Scattered as they are between the jogging trails and free speech zones, the small groves of synthetics are nothing like this living, breathing forest sprawled beyond the window. A wonder of the natural world. She would call it magical if she didn't know better.

Magic is anything but wonderful.

"I gotta hand it to him. Kyle did pretty damn good."

"Okay, your brother gets points for location, but I'm still not looking forward to freezing my butt off."

Another car pulls up behind them as Sebastian turns off the ignition. It's half the size of Sebastian's truck, baby blue, with rainbow bumper stickers all across the front and back. How their friends survived the long drive in Javier's tiny smart compact without killing each other is beyond her.

Sebastian leans over the center console and nuzzles her ear with his nose. "Don't worry, baby. I'll keep you warm."

"Yeah, I bet you will."

Lascivious bastard.

Giggling with delight as his breath tickles her neck, she ducks away, slipping off her seatbelt and stepping out of the car. A shiver rockets up her legs as her bare ankles meet the cool autumn air. It was a warm 75 degrees when they left the little highway hotel where they spent the night, but that was at five o'clock in the morning. They've been on the road for nearly ten hours, and while she did change into warmer jeans and a long–sleeved shirt at the last rest stop, she didn't change her shoes. A pair of knee–high stockings and her favorite pair of hiking boots are calling her name from the back of the truck.

"Didn't you used to spend weeks at a time out in the wilderness? You told me your instructors once dropped you in the middle of the desert with nothing but a backpack and a map and told you to find your way back. What's a few nights in the woods with lots of gear compared to that?"

"I was seventeen and training to be a technomancer, Sebastian. It's been nearly seven years."

Seven years since Lily tried and failed to pass the 247th Technomancer Trials. She isn't bitter about it; she flunked out on a stupid alchemical theorem! She'd even been invited to try again the following year, but then the world went to hell in a handbasket as Seraphim opened fire on pretty much every other League nation. Because of it, however, the trials were halted for two years, and by the time they started back up, well... let's just say her health disqualified her from participating.

It's fine. She doesn't miss the lifestyle. Aighneas keeps a militarized training regimen for their human+ trainees, and while she does miss wearing the uniform from time to time, not having to wake up at an ungodly 4AM every morning is utter bliss. Oh, and being able to wear make–up whenever the fuck she wants is a bonus. Besides, she's pursuing other career opportunities. Or maybe she should say other "educational" opportunities? "Career" implies she's done anything other than go to school the last six years of her life.

"You realize my thesis is due in less than a month, right?"

"And you said you didn't want to work on it this weekend because you wanted to enjoy the holiday."

Sebastian has a career.

He's a kindergarten teacher at a local elementary school. They met almost two years ago, completely by chance, when Lily was monitoring one of her student teachers from the university. As the youngest doctoral student in the department, she'd drawn the short straw to supervise the undergrad students trying for their teaching certification.

"You said *you* didn't want to work this weekend. I merely hummed in agreement, thinking I'd be left in peace to do my work."

She doesn't even like Halloween or Hexennacht or Samhain whatever you want to call it. It's a holiday for hexen. Humans just hate missing out on an opportunity to get drunk and stupid.

"The fresh air will be good for you," continues Sebastian as he helps her into a thick thermal coat. "You've spent so much time buried in your hub, you've started growing mushrooms on your head."

"I have not!"

He catches her by the hip, dodging her slap and tugging her in close despite the hiking pack in her arms. For a normal, Sebastian is strong. He winks down at her with a twinkle in his eye. Lily's neural hub immediately goes into overdrive trying to cool her down as a blush rises to her cheeks.

"Hey," he says with his winning smile. "You remember what you told your undergrads about Hexennacht, right?"

"That it's a rip–off of some old–world holiday called Halloween, and that it's the reason so many children need dentures before their adult teeth come in."

"I don't remember that being part of Professor Albridge's curriculum," pipes up Javier, stepping out of the passenger seat of the little blue smartie. Javier is one of Lily's cohorts, and the first real friend she made after entering civie life. He swaggers his way toward the bickering couple like some varsity sportsman, though he's never played a day in his life. "I have a delicate disposition," he'd use as an excuse whenever she tried to get him to play holo ball with her at the campus gym—a sport which, by the way, is basically a virtual version of ping pong.

So yeah. Suffice to say: Sports + Javi = NO.

Unless someone was talking about a rigorous game of chess—that's an entirely different story. He's been toting around his recent championship cup the way a wrestler wears their heavyweight belts, hips cocked forward, shoulders back, and throwing elbows even though his noodly arms couldn't shove an overweight guinea pig out of his way. Despite his miraculous ability to carry around at least twenty books at a time, all of Javier's brawn is in his brains. Why he said yes to Sebastian's asinine weekend getaway is lost on her. You'd think he would much rather stay home and play video games over the weekend with his husband.

"Well, Professor Albridge isn't here to correct me, now is she? Besides, while she's on sabbatical, I'm teaching the class, and I don't teach nonsense."

Javier shakes his head at her, curly brown locks bouncing. How is it men manage to have such luscious hair without even trying?

"Hexen Anthropology, right?" Javier's tall, dark, and buff husband Derrick comes around, carrying his and Javier's tent kit.

Where Javier is the epitome of a noodle, Derrick is a perfectly cooked steak. Tall with hazel–hued, deep brown skin, Derrick is a personal trainer and a bodybuilder who enjoys his weekends LARPing with a group of cosplayers as Rahad the wizard. He even keeps a full beard perfectly groomed for the appearance of looking like a wizened sage. "100% home grown!" He likes to crow whenever he's flexing, but she's never really sure if he's talking about his muscles or his facial hair. Not that either is something to shake a feather at. His beard is as luxurious as a lion's mane, partially braided and beaded, well–oiled, and meticulously combed, and his biceps are the size of Lily's head. But for all his ferocious appearance, he's a total sweetie, doting on Javier whenever he can.

"I remember taking that class as an elective in undergrad. My favorite unit was the one on Halloween myths and legends—how they shape the way we celebrate Hexennacht today."

"Yup. That's why she only offers the class in the fall," replies Javier as his husband folds him into an oversized coat. Javier rises onto the balls of his feet to adjust the colorful pompom–peaked knit hat atop Derrick's bald head, making sure it is centered rather than hanging over his ear. Javier slaved over his knitting needles in the grad office for a whole week, trying to finish it by Derrick's last birthday. Amidst midterms, while Lily had been slammed with students complaining about their grades, Javier's students gave the knitting man a wide berth, probably too afraid of flying needles to risk stressing the grad out any further.

"You don't understand how jealous I am that they assigned the class to you. All they gave me was Old World Anthro."

"They gave me the class because my thesis is on hexen rumors and superstitions. Yours is on the cultural shifts that took place between the A.D. and A.P. eras and how Old–World cultures evolved upon transition to Deus."

"Yeah, I know, but you could at least keep some of her traditions. The best part about being her TA was getting to wear costumes the whole Month of Darkness."

"That's because Hexennacht is your favorite holiday for some unholy reason." Jeanine, Javier's sister, steps out of the backseat wearing a fur–lined black coat with a hot pink backpack, better suited for school textbooks than a camping trip, slung over one shoulder. Between her long sheet of black hair and powdered skin, she looks like a pre–Gomez, co–ed version of Morticia Addams.

"Like you aren't the freak who starts decorating three months early," Javier says.

"What can I say? My aesthetic is spooky and pink."

"Yes, and you keep that vibe going all the way through New Year's."

Jeanine pulls the lower lid of her right eye down and sticks her tongue out at her older brother. "It's the Nightmare Before Yule, not the Night, and bats are so much cuter than turtle doves."

Javier just rolls his eyes, turning the topic back to Hexennacht.

"There's a myth that a lost spirit might find you, banish your soul into the underworld, and take possession of your body. That's why organics and posties are supposed to dress up on Hexennacht so the spirits don't recognize you as human."

"It's strange how most people decide to dress up as hexen or fae though. Why not just be an animal of some kind? We're supposed to be scared of witches, but they sell witch hats everywhere during the Month of Darkness."

"That's the point, Jeanine. They're scary. You want to frighten away the ghosts."

"I heard it was so doppelgangers can't steal your identity," laughs Sebastian.

Derrick holds his hands up. "Whoa, whoa, whoa. Hold the spooky stories. I didn't pack a costume."

"Oh, Derrick," teases Javier. "You overgrown chicken."

"My sorority sisters and I were planning on having a spooky movie marathon," whines Jeanine. "Yet here I am with you losers."

Javier makes a face at his sister.

"It's not like anyone made you come."

"And let you get yourself killed on a Hexennacht camping trip? Do you realize how horror movie cliché that is? If you wanted to get scared, we could have gone to a haunted house or something. There's a really spooky one held by Alpha Kappa Psi every year."

"Eew! Who wants to pay to have a bunch of horror–obsessed frat boys grope you?"

"They don't grope you, Derrick."

"Last year I got groped, and I will swear on it until the day I die."

"Yeah, whatever."

"Another one," continues Javier, "says the reason we give out candy is because vampyres won't drink your blood if there's too much sugar in it."

"You mean," inserts Sebastian, "they won't drink the blood of people dying from alcohol poisoning."

Actually, the blood–alcohol myth isn't a myth at all, and fairly practical, if Lily's reasoning is correct. If alcohol can fuck up a living person's system that badly, what do you think it'll do to someone without a fully functioning liver?

"My favorite is the one about the three old crones who came back to life only to die again at sunrise because they were outsmarted by a bunch of teenagers. There's a talking cat and everything in it."

"You're such a geek, *mi amor*," says Javier, leaning up to kiss Derrick on his whiskered cheek.

"That's a movie, not a legend," says Lily. "People coming back to life is a bunch of hocus pocus. It's not possible, and whatever stories you're thinking of, stop—95% of those stories are utter crock."

"Says Miss–I–once–trained–under–The–Morrigan," sing-songs Jeanine, one hip cocked to the side. "Of course, you're going to tell us not to put any stock in it. But you must admit, there's a granule of truth in every story."

"And usually that truth is 'it's an utter lie.' I thought I made that clear to you guys last week in class."

The undergrad is a regular to Lily's tutoring sessions, pre-ferring hers to her brother's for some odd reason. When the twenty–one–year old isn't spending time with her sorority sisters, she is avidly studying hexen as much as anyone out-side of the League's adept and technomancer program is allowed to study. She jokes about her love of the topic, saying she just wants to marry a technomancer one day by getting a research position in the government, but Lily knows she enjoys the topic.

"Yes, yes, and never forget you can't spell 'believe' without the word 'lie.' I remember."

"Correct. Real hexen tales are not jokes to be taken lightly. They aren't fairy tales you can turn into kiddy films where animals sing, and all the princess loses is a shoe. Professor Albridge's class is only allowed to be taught on the grounds that everything is framed by historical curiosity, nothing else." Not to mention, it doesn't hold a candle to the things she learned as an adept. "We read those texts to understand hexen thinking, protect ourselves against them, and for those of us capable, kill hexen. You'd be more frightened of them if you ever actually met a witch."

"Yeah, well the chance of that ever happening is pretty slim, don't 'cha think, Lil?"

Lily's shoulders sag. *Yeah...Especially now* she's *gone...*

"But you're writing your dissertation on hexen folklore?" asks Javier.

"Not exactly. I'm doing my research on the myths and rumors surrounding the Songstress of Lorelei. And even if

I was, folklore is just that: folk*LORE*! None of it is real. Like the urban legend about pop rocks bursting in your stomach if you eat them with soda."

"Or hair growing on your palm if you—"

"Gross, Derrick."

"Anyway," inserts Sebastian loudly, stretching the vowels out with a long aaah, "I'm not talking about the mumbo jumbo we teach five–year–olds to get them to behave. I'm talking about what you told me last year. People used to believe the veil between the living and the dead is thinnest on Halloween. The legend says too much celebration can rouse the ghosts of recently deceased witches at the witching hour."

"Sebastian..."

"They originally wanted to jump all of the clocks forward an hour at 3AM, but with the different time zones it didn't seem like a logical solution, so instead the League installed a mandatory curfew on All Hallow's Eve because they're afraid people will disturb the ghost of the Songstress of Lorelei."

Derrick crosses himself and Javier pales.

"Good thing we came to the middle of nowhere to party," drawls Jeanine. "That way no one can hear us screaming when we accidentally summon a vengeful witch from the dead."

"No one is summoning a witch anywhere." Lily glares at Sebastian, who holds up his hands in defense. "There is no truth to that legend. Anyone who says otherwise doesn't know what they're talking about, and we will not be looking for the opportunity to test it."

"Of course, baby. Sorry. I was just thinking about that story."

"Well, stop thinking about it before I knock it out of your brain. Ghosts and witch spirits. What a load of crock!"

This seems to quell Derrick's rising panic, and the color returns to Javier's cheeks.

"I thought you said your brother was bringing us on a ghost tour?"

Sebastian laughs, shifting from one foot to the other. "My brother just thinks this place is cool enough to attract tourists. Kyle's ghost tours are always gags and money scams. None of it is actually scary, and there are certainly never any real ghosts. This is an autumn camping trip that just so happens to fall on Hexennacht."

"Good," huffs Lily, crossing her arms. "The last thing I need is to be stuck in the middle of nowhere *and* surrounded by ghosts."

"Right, just some good, old–fashioned camping. Glad you're coming around to the idea."

His sarcasm is unamusing, so Lily shakes her head and goes to fish the rest of her gear out of the truck bed.

"I am not coming around to the idea. I thought we would be going to a lodge or something, not walking into the woods in the middle of nowhere where I can't get a connection."

"Babe, I'm sorry I wasn't clear, but that's the whole point of camping. Disconnecting and getting away from the stressors of regular life. You can't do that at a lodge where the television sions are always turned on to the news."

Lily huffs, letting her duffle plop to the ground by a tire.

He doesn't understand. He isn't augmented. Not like she is. This far away from the city, she is completely disconnected from the network. When Sebastian told her they would be going glamping, she imagined paying to sleep outside some swanky resort where the bathrooms were just a stone's throw away, the WIFI had a password, and her comm units were still a viable means of communication. Instead, she's found herself in a dead zone.

"Where are we anyway?"

"You mean you don't know with all of that high quality tech in your head?"

"Do I look like a GPS? You were driving, and you purposely went out of your way to keep this as mysterious as possible, and unfortunately, I tend to make the mistake of trusting you far more often than I should."

"Hmm, you really shouldn't do that," he teases back, winking at her good–naturedly, the man already moving past their little pseudo spat despite her lingering ire. He's lucky he has a great smile. The cleft chin gives him an unfair advantage. Otherwise, she just might've punched him. It helps that she kinda loves him, too. Just kinda.

Lily rises onto her toes as he leans down, but just as they are about to kiss, the loud roar of a 10–cylinder engine pulls up.

11

Lucy in the Sky with Diamonds

"SERIOUSLY, BASSY. ALREADY MAKING IT with your honey? We just got here!"

Lily bites down the groan threatening to rumble out of her throat. It's Kyle, Sebastian's older brother. Hard–assed, boot-wearing Kyle who is as dark as his brother is golden. Perpetually red–faced with dark, sunburnt auburn hair and darker brown eyes, they could pass as twins were it not for the opposing color schemes of their hair and eyes. They have the same winning dimpled smile, albeit Kyle's is marred by the ever–present bulge of chewing tobacco in his cheek.

"Lily's not my 'honey,' Ky. She's my girlfriend. There's a difference."

The heavy titanium of Kyle's mechanical arm catches the sunlight, reflecting right into Lily's eye as he shuts off the bike. The keyring makes a harsh scratchy sound as he twirls it around a steel finger. Kyle is augmented, not in the same way Lily is, but he has a mechanical right arm—the result of a chance encounter with a lycan. The bite had been high up on his arm, bisecting his bicep, and the protocol is a full amputation two to four inches proximal to the heart from the bite depending on time since attack to prevent the spread of the curse. The whole limb was lost as a result, but he makes do with his prosthesis and calls himself a cyborg even though he only has the one augmentation.

Legally, someone can only declare cyborgian status in Aighneas if they are in possession of a minimum of three augmentations necessary to sensory ability and/or mobility like hearing aids or mechanical limbs. The exception to this is if for people in possession of an augmentation they would die without.

Someone like Lily with a synthetic nervous system.

Lily may not look it, but she's got far more tech running through her body than he: muscle enhancements, skeletal plating, a toxicity filtration system, oxygen optimizations, and most notable, her neural net, her cerebral connection to the cyberscape, indicated by the circular hub high on the back of her neck. (An implant she's had since she was eight years old.) She used to have an offensive system in her left forearm, complete with a high–density laser, but after resigning from the military, she replaced it with a basic utility system complete with a pocketknife, screwdriver, corkscrew, and flashlight.

"Not from where I'm standing." Kyle laughs, one eyebrow cocked skyward. "You two looking mighty cozy. How ya doing, Lil? My little bro been keeping all 'em hidden buttons of yours fine–tuned?"

She doesn't appreciate the lewdness of the question or the dig at her augmentations.

"What can I say? He's good with his hands," she says, aiming a winning grin at Kyle as if she was shooting a laser at a target drone. "Better than any mechanic I've ever met. Knows just how to make my motors purr. Hope you don't mind the noise. Oh wait, your arm is so noisy I can hear it creaking a mile away, so that shouldn't be a problem."

The man grunts in admiration of her come back and shoves his flesh hand in his pocket.

"Don't worry. I'll be sure to set up my tent far away from yours. Provided of course you didn't lose any of the equipment I put in your truck."

And why he couldn't drive his own shit here, Lily hasn't the slightest idea.

"Why don't you check for yourself, you rusty piece of junk?" Sebastian throws back with a smile, greeting his brother with a handshake and a chest bump.

"Jerk! I've been driving all day. You gonna make me start lugging hiking equipment around already?"

"You could've ridden with us, Kyle," calls Jeanine.

"Right...and listen to you chatter on about the latest episode of *Gossip+ Girl* while the married couple makes kissy faces at each other for more than twelve hours."

Javier and Derrick look sidelong at each other while Jeanine rolls her eyes.

"Dude, we've been married for two years, not two weeks."

"I mean, we like each other, but we're not newlyweds."

"Yeah, sure. I believe you. Hey, Bassy, give me the keys. I need to stretch my legs."

Sebastian tosses his keys to his brother.

"Right on. Let me get my shit, and we can hit the trail."

The man treks around to the back of Sebastian's truck. Lily visibly sags as he leaves. She doesn't dislike Kyle, but she doesn't particularly enjoy sharing space with him either.

"So, are you going to tell me where we are?"

"Absolutely!" Sebastian wraps an arm around her shoulder and tucks her into his side. "We are in Blackwood Forest."

"But Blackwood is a pine forest, isn't it? This is a broadleaf forest."

"That's what Kyle told me. He showed me pictures of where we're going. There's a lake and a cabin and an amazing view of the mountains. You're gonna love it."

"Dragging me all the way out to the middle of nowhere? I had better love it."

Otherwise, she just might make him sleep outside the tent. Maybe a spider will bite him in the ass.

It's not long before Lily finds out why Kyle couldn't pack his own equipment into his truck.

"Tada!"

He pulls the tarp off to reveal a brand–new carriage droid painted in a green and blue camouflage. Round bodied with a cubicle–like sensory cam for a head, it looks a little like a turtle with a flat shell. It even has four miniature engines equidistant from each other around the body to help it hover off the ground.

"May I present the top–of–the–line KC–4M19?"

Kyle picks up a remote and flips the switch. The droid revs to life with a series of multi–tonal beeps and clicks, fancy lights flickering on in vibrant greens and blues—installed for pure aesthetic. The droid is roughly the size of a child's play wagon, and with a puff of steam, it rises off the bed of the truck and zips its way over the tailgate to hover a good foot above the dirt ground.

"Now we won't need to lug all of our shit around. We can put most of it on KC here."

"She is so cute!" Jeanine squeals, running over to put her hand on KC's "head." The little camera swivels and a scanner pans over her face.

"*He* is not cute."

"Robots are usually referred to as female, Kyle."

"Yeah, well KC is a hard–working bot. Ain't got time to be called 'cute' by nobody."

"Well, *she's* cuter than you. That's for sure."

Kyle looks at the co–ed in faux hurt before giving her a smirk. "Welp, guess he's only going to be carrying my stuff then."

"Wait, no. I take it back. KC can be a 'he.'"

Fifteen minutes later, they're trekking their way through the forest, Kyle at the helm and KC buzzing along behind them carrying Jeanine and Javier's backpacks along with a small supply of foodstuffs, a cooler, and camping equipment. It skims across the uneven ground and debris of the forest floor as easily as a hoverboard over cement. Lily has to hand it to Kyle: the little drone was a great idea for this trip. They'll be able to move faster and take more with them into the woods. Only an hour into their trek and already they are surrounded by forest. Were it not for her internal compass, Lily would have no idea which direction to go to get back to the cars.

"This place is amazing. Can you imagine hosting a tournament in these woods?"

Derrick, fantasizing about his next LARPing adventure, is not wrong.

The forest thrums with life and unfettered, wild magic, and she doesn't need her scanners to tell her as much. She can feel it in the ground under her feet, in the trees around her, the bones of the world vibrating with power, and unlike most places where magic still lives, this forest does not slumber. In the short time they've been walking, they've passed a burrow of rabbits, countless birds, and a small herd of deer with their fawns grazing in the grass. None of the animals react to their presence, entirely unconditioned to fear them, carrying on with their day as though there weren't a bunch of noisy people traipsing through their woods. A fox catches a pigeon, the birds sing their evening anthems, and a squirrel scurries up a tree with a prized acorn between its teeth.

The vitality of nature in action.

"Rahad would totally hunker down in one of these trees," Derrick says, gesturing toward a thick evergreen, "and chuck fireballs at all of the poor paladins trying to clip–clop their way to glory. What do you think, babe? Should I make a proposal to the committee? Change the venue for the next tourney?"

Lily doesn't say it aloud, but Derrick's idea may very well have him and anyone else foolish enough to try and invade this place falling asleep in a fairy ring, doomed to never wake again and dance themselves to death.

You don't go traipsing into woods like this to play foolish games. Kyle had better know what the hell he's doing bringing them to a place like this.

"I don't think so, *mi amor*. Didn't you say they were planning the next tourney for the Month of Ice? It'll be way too cold by then, and as much as I love you, I am not wearing long johns just because you want to go LARPing."

"Baby, don't worry. I'll keep you plenty warm. No long johns required."

"Gross, you two!"

Jeanine makes a gagging face as Derrick plants a wet one on Javier's cheek. Javier winks at his sister, hand thrown up in a lewd gesture.

Lily just shakes her head. Let them be as sickeningly sweet as they like. They've worked too long and too hard for their relationship—they deserve to make everyone around them puke if they want to—and Lily will tell them to go puke elsewhere if they have a problem with it.

"Speaking of sleeping in long johns, are we planning to stop soon? It's getting dark."

And the temperature is dropping. Lily rubs her hands together in a vain attempt to warm them. How could she have forgotten her damned gloves in the truck? And her toes are starting to go numb, too.

"Don't you have body temp regulators somewhere in all of those fancy tech systems?" Kyle laughs.

"No, BTRs are technomancer–grade augmentations."

"Oh, right, and you flunked out."

"She didn't flunk out, Kyle."

Sebastian mouths "don't listen to him" to her behind Kyle's back, tacking on a cross–eyed, tongue–out, wacky face to the end that never fails to make Lily laugh. He even adds a rotating finger to his temple pointing in his big brother's direction for added insult.

"Well, she sure as hell didn't pass either. And lucky you for that misfortune. You think she'd be dating your sorry ass if she had?"

Talk about a backwards compliment...

Javier separates from Derrick, turning and walking backward with his hands on his hips. "And you think you could've passed, hotshot?"

"I sure as hell have a better chance at it than you."

"I'm not going to argue that, but those trials are no joke. People die during them, and it's not Lily's fault she got sick after—Ah!"

With a sharp snap, Javier tumbles sideways.

"Javi!" Derrick cries out as his husband rolls head over heels backward down the steep slope, his limbs and body meeting various trees during his descent before he lands in a puddle of groans and bruises at the bottom of the ravine.

Derrick takes off after his husband, the others not far behind.

"Javi?"

"Ughhh..."

Derrick drops to his knees next to a wincing but awake Javier.

"Hey, booboo, what hurts? Talk to me."

"M–my ankle. Ow!" he shouts, trying to move it. "Goddamnit... Why does this always happen to me? We've only been in the woods for two hours."

Derrick wipes the tears from Javier's eyes, cleaning up the mud now caked to his face.

"That brain of yours is just too much for your body to handle. That's why you're so clumsy. It runs so fast your feet can't keep up."

"Yeah, neither can his mouth."

Kyle ambles his way down and taps Javier's ankle. Predictably, Javier whimpers like a kicked puppy.

"Great! Just great!" Kyle throws his arms in the air, then crosses them as he stands over their injured friend. "We'll have to take him back to the trucks. Cancel your little Halloween party, folks, because we're marching right back home."

Javier looks up, wide-eyed, glasses askew on his face.

"Wait, no! It's just twisted. See—I can walk. We don't need to go back."

Despite the protests of his husband and sister, Javier tries to stand up only to crumple back to the ground in a heap when his ankle fails to hold his weight.

"Fuck!"

"Yeah," gruffs Kyle. "Like I said, we'll have to carry him back. So much for a fucking camping trip."

"Can't KC carry him?" asks Jeanine. "Then we can keep on going."

"The drone can't lift more than a hundred pounds, so no. We'll have to do it ourselves. Glad you decided to lay off the cheeseburgers, babe."

"Don't be a dick, Kyle."

Lily shoulders her way past Sebastian's brother to Javier. "Here. Don't move. I have a medi-stim."

Lily drops her pack to the floor and yanks open the center zipper.

"You have a what?"

"A medi-stim. They're adept-grade first aid. It's basically an injection of nano-bots. They'll enter your bloodstream and heal you from the inside."

"Whoa, whoa, whoa—a bunch of mini-robots zooming through my insides?"

"Think of them like a bunch of micro–constructions workers moving in to repair the damage to a building before it needs to be condemned."

Javier's eyes, magnified by his glasses, are round with fright. It's so adorable, Lily wants to wrap him in a hug. He clearly watches too many science fiction movies, gory things made by producers who just love to splash a bit of blood on a couple of batteries, computers, and wires and paint portraits of cyborgean horror to the terror of normals everywhere.

"Is it safe?"

"It's perfectly safe. I've used them dozens of times. The nanos'll flush out of your bloodstream in 24 hours, and it'll take less than that to fix up a twisted ankle."

Javier's eyes shift from Lily to Derrick for reassurance—"You'll be fine, booboo"—and back.

"What do you think? Yes or no?"

Javier nods, hissing when the needle goes in. The injection is barely a sting, Lily knows from experience, little more than a mosquito bite without the lingering itch; though, she supposes for a normal it might leave a bit of an uncomfortable bump.

"Umm, Lily?"

Sebastian.

"Yeah, babe?"

"You didn't tell me you brought like hi–tech stuff."

Hi-tech stuff? It's just a medical stim. They're a basic first aid item. You'd be a fool to forget bringing at least one on a mission. Technomancers are as much an investment to the League as they are weapons. As such, they're expected to keep themselves alive by any means. Even trainees were hardly allowed to leave base without at least one or two in their kits.

"I told you I brought first aid supplies."

"You consider medi–stims first aid?" asks Kyle.

Lily turns to Kyle in confusion.

"Well, yeah. You don't spend years of your life in military training and forget to implement the most basic of rules. Lionheart once got a write up as a recruit when he forgot his stim on a training excavation."

"Baby, those things cost like five hundred a pop."

She freezes.

Oh, right. She'd forgotten. They're civilians. In Aighneas, nanotech including medi–stims are military exclusive unless you are willing to pay an arm and a leg for them as a private citizen. Lily, ex–military as she is, is not just allowed to have them but the maintenance required of her augmentations requires her usage of them lest she risk disintegration, rejection, or ultimately death due to a frayed wire.

"I have access to them because of my status as a cyborg and my contacts with the military."

To Sebastian's left, Jeanine shifts uneasily from foot to foot, casting odd glances toward Lily. With the growing darkness, the lights in her eyes must be visible. Unlike the sights of the Miyazaki family and Muraskan technomancers, hers don't turn off. They remain perpetually lit, a faint red glow at the very center of her pupil.

"I didn't realize you still had connections with the military."

"I was augmented as a child by the military. I may not be considered military personnel anymore, but I still have responsibilities, and without the various nano injections, my tech system could collapse. I've told you this."

Who does he think is paying for her degree?

"I guess I didn't realize you still received nano–tech from them."

"Well, I don't care why or how you have it because, holy shit, I feel good."

The group laughs at Javier's dreamy proclamation.

The man is on cloud 9, eyes dilated, jaw slack, head lolling to the side, and he won't be coming down anytime soon. She'd forgotten how normals respond to stims, the strange mix of high and low incited by them. Some normals become high as a kite; others drop into the deepest of despair; others still experience the most extreme swings from one end to the other, manic in its polarizations of behavior. Derrick helps Javier stand, not that he needs the help. He practically leaps up onto his feet. Once he gets there, though, he makes the mistake of putting his full weight on his injured ankle.

"Ow!!" he moans, teetering sideways into Derrick.

"Don't get too excited. That's just the painkiller talking. You'll still need a couple of hours for the nanos to repair your ankle before you can walk right again."

"So still a gimp then. Got it."

"Just for a little while."

"We should set up camp for the night," suggests Jeanine, flipping her ponytail over.

"Not here," gruffs Kyle. "This is a ravine. If it rains, we'll end up flooded out. We'll go back up the hill to higher ground."

"Whatever you say, boss." Sebastian claps Kyle on the shoulder before ducking down to slide under Javier's other arm. Then he helps trudge Javier out of the ditch with Derrick. Meanwhile, Kyle chews the dip in his mouth, spits a black globule on the ground, offers Lily's look of disgust a winning smirk, and follows.

Jeanine shrugs.

"At least he doesn't carry around a gross bottle of spit."

"You'd think he would know better. Nicotine doesn't meld well with neuropozyne."

Jeanine laughs.

"You know. I find it hard to believe those two are related sometimes. They're so different."

Sebastian's seen his share of struggles. He moved away from his family to go to college despite his dad busting his ass about going into the family business of swindling people for a living. Kyle, on the other hand... Lily's met a lot of men like Kyle. You meet them in the ranks of adept trainees all the time. Men with glory fever in their veins. Men looking for fresh meat to rend, men looking for a fight, men looking for a license to kill.

"Yeah, I know." Lily shoulders her pack, stepping back toward KC, hovering on the lip of the ravine and seemingly waiting for them. "Come on. Let's not let the boys leave us ladies behind."

"Oh, please. You and I both know they would die without us."

The girls' laughter rings through the trees as the sun lowers, streaking the sky through with the most brilliant shades of orange, red, and purple, and the whole forest goes up in the cool flames of a shifting of season.

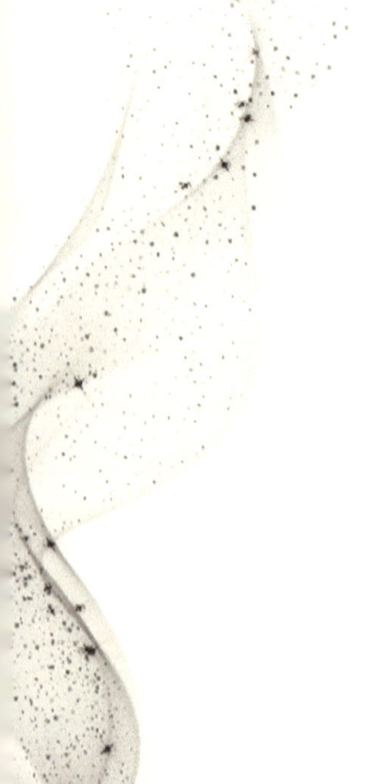

III

The Witching Hour

THWACK!

"You have an axe?"

Kyle twirls the weapon with an utterly blasé attitude, Javier flinching into Derrick despite being a good four feet out of range. The hatchet spins like a top as it leaves his robotic hand before catching it deftly, the business end pointed toward the closest tree trunk.

"Of course, I have an axe. You think I'm going to go into the woods without a means to clear a path or chop firewood? If we were in the jungle, I'd've packed a machete."

With one mech–handed swing, he embeds the axe into the wood with a heavy thwack. The thunk reverberates in Lily's bones, and when he swings again, this time down toward the base of a thick branch, the limb collapses, splintering from its trunk. The leaves rustle and whine as they hit the ground, narrowly avoiding Derrick and Javier's freshly erected tent.

"Hey, Ky, easy with that axe. You nearly hit Derrick and Javier's tent."

"Sorry, Bassy." He throws a wink at Sebastian, not sounding repentant at all.

Javier huffs, leaning into Derrick.

"Do we really want the metal man swinging an axe around?"

"Javi, don't call him metal man. He's augmented, not a robot."

"You sure? Seems to me like his skull is made of metal too and quite hollow."

"You want to take a swing, chess master?" Javier's shoulders rise in alarm as Kyle addresses him with a guffaw. "Oh wait, you can't! No thanks to that ankle of yours. Hell, you've probably got more robotics swimming around in your bloodstream than me right now thanks to Lily's little medi–stim. Hahaha. 'Metal man.' I like that, dude. Maybe it'll be my next tattoo."

The axe hits the tree with another thwack.

"Kyle," Jeanine protests. "Can we not rip the forest to pieces?"

"You want a fire or not? Because I sure as fuck ain't keeping you warm tonight. Not unless you ask real nicely."

Thwack!

Another branch tumbles down.

"Yuck, you perv. I just don't think we should be cutting down trees. It seems... I don't know. Disrespectful."

"They're plants. They aren't owed respect."

Thwack! The crunch of leaves.

Thwack! The scream of bark.

"Alright!" shouts Lily. "I think we have plenty of wood."

"Aww, but I was just getting my gait right."

"I'm sure your form is fine. This is too much as it is. We can't exactly burn whole branches. You can chop up what's already on the ground."

"Spoilsport."

"Kyle," chides Sebastian.

"Alright, alright. I'm done." He whacks the axe into the thick trunk of the maple tree he just hacked up and leaves it there. "Bunch of piss–buckets."

The man marches off into the forest with a half–hearted proclamation of taking a walk around the area, telling Sebastian to get a fire going while he's gone. How Sabastian manages to understand his brother is a mystery to Lily. Every other word is a spat curse.

With a shrug and a sigh, Sebastian rises from anchoring their tent and makes his way to the axe embedded in the tree trunk. He grasps the handle with both hands and tugs. The hatchet doesn't move, it's buried so deep into the tree.

Derrick whistles lowly, impressed. "Anger management much?"

"Derrick," chides Javier.

"What? It's true. Here, mate. Let me give you a hand."

The two tug at the axe together, yet still it doesn't budge—stuck fast. After a while, they give up, Derrick turning to Javier.

"Hey baby, what was the name of the sword in the stone?"

"Excalibur?"

"More like Axe–calibur."

Lily rolls her eyes as they give up, choosing instead to break off smaller branches by hand. Before long, Derrick and Sebastian have a gently crackling fire built up in the center of their camp.

"Ooh, you know what would be perfect?" Jeanine smiles over the mug of her hot cocoa, eyes sparking in the light of the fire. "Scary stories around the campfire. Anybody know any?"

"Oh, no, no, no, no, no." Derrick waves his hands in the air in front of him, flicking his beard the way a model would her hair. "I am not about the Are–You–Afraid–of–the–Dark bullshit. No, no, no."

"Aww, baby. They're just stories."

Javier winds his arms around Derrick's middle, laughing at the taller man's distress.

"And all stories are rooted in some insidious truth, and I ain't about that life."

"Oh, just one, Derrick. I promise it won't be bad."

"Are you going to tell it?"

Javier blushes. "Um, well. I don't know any."

"Exactly."

"Do you know any Hexennacht stories, Sebastian?"

Sebastian shakes his head.

"Not any scary ones. Just the kind you read to five– and six– year–olds. You know, talking black cats, magical pumpkins, and friendly neighborhood sheet ghosts."

"Bummer." Jeanine wilts. "I don't know any, either."

"I know one."

They turn to Lily, Jeanine and Javier looking like eager school children while Derrick and Sebastian both look about ready to run for the hills.

"It's called—"

"Wait, wait, wait. Before you start, you need a flashlight."

Javier digs a torch out of his backpack and tosses it to Lily, who clicks the light on and dramatically tilts it under her chin. Her cheeks become gaunt and hollow, her eyes hooded and black, and her brow disappears into the shadows.

"Spooky enough for you now?"

A chorus of "woos" comes from her friends. Even KC gives an appreciative "beep beep," the little drone resting on the ground. Sebastian takes a drink from his water canteen and nudges her hip.

"Do your worst, babe."

"You sure, honey? I might make you cry."

"So long as you promise to tuck me in when I go to bed."

Bony fingers dig into her sides again, making her howl with laughter, and she gives him back just as good.

"Ow, babe! Your nails are sharp."

"Then don't tickle me!"

He goes down laughing as she shoves him off the end of the log. Javier gives Derrick a conspiratorial glance.

"And people say we're bad?"

"Any day, you two."

Dusting the dirt off his trousers, Sebastian reclaims his spot next to Lily, tucking an arm around her waist.

"Sorry, sorry. I'll behave," he says, planting a chilly kiss on her cheek. His lips are already chapped from the frosty air, and she wonders if he brought chapstick.

"Should we wait for Kyle?"

"Nah, he wouldn't appreciate it. Go ahead. He'll come back when he comes back."

"Okay." Lily clears her throat and settles back in her seat. "I give you The Eerie Old Tale on Eerie Lane Brook."

"Nice." Despite his earlier reluctance for scary stories, Derrick rubs his hands together eagerly.

"At the edge of Eerie Lane Brook before there even was an Eerie Lane Brook, there was a wise old redwood that stood watch over the forest for decades, possibly even centuries. It was said a forest sprite lived in the tree and would grant wishes to any and all who came to find her, provided of course they brought with them an offering that brought her great pleasure, and yes, I do mean *that* kind of pleasure."

Lily grins coyly. Jeanine giggles while Javier whispers to Derrick, "Guess we won't be qualifying."

"One day, however, a businessman came sniffing about. Paul Cartridge's dream was to build the perfect home, smart and fully automated, and he just so happened to want to build the house right where the ancient tree stood erect for so long, so of course, without any regard for the old tree or the legends surrounding it, he chopped it down."

"Sound familiar to anyone?" drones Javier.

"Shh!"

"The locals warned Paul against this. They claimed the tree was a guardian spirit, magical and effervescent, and the reason they all benefited from the good fortunes of fine weather, plentiful harvest, and profitable business ventures. To cut it down would be to bring a fate worse than death upon him. Needless to say, he didn't listen, but he didn't waste the wood, either. He used it to build his house. The stairway, the banister, the floorboards, and the most essential part of his home: his computing hub. A magnificent operating desk inlaid with a high–powered motherboard and holo–projection nodes. The brain center of his home, the cerebellum and cerebrum all wrapped up in one pristine room where he could immerse himself in the cyberscape and ensure his family (Dorine, his beautiful wife, and teenage son, Jimmy) never wanted for anything."

The howl of a great wolf sings through the night. Derrick and Jeanine both tense, looking toward the sound.

Lily turns back to the group and continues her story.

"Once the house was built, he moved his family into their new home, and for a while, everything was fine. The businessman would kiss his wife goodbye before going to work every day, Jimmy started going to school, and the wife began to get to know the neighborhood housewives. A quaint perfect little existence in a house that knew their every want before they could even want for it.

"But then strange things began to happen. Nothing outright alarming. The toaster would burn Dorine's toast, the television would lose signal, the window blinds would open and close uncommanded. For the longest time, Paul chalked it up to a bug in the system, working tirelessly to solve the problem, but every time he squashed one bug, another would crop up, even worse than the last. Hot water outages during Dorine's spa days, electricity failures during the World Cup, and worst of all, the internet disconnecting during Jimmy's online games."

"Dun, dun, dun!"

The boys laugh at Sebastian's sound effects. The girls just roll their eyes

"Now, Jimmy was a very curious child. He enjoyed reading comic books and playing video games, and his favorite place to play games was on his dad's hub. The network was fast, when the internet wasn't down, and the graphics were state of the art, but his dad didn't like him playing in his office, especially with all of the strange occurrences happening. The last thing Paul needed was another firewall going down, and the last time Jimmy used his hub, one of the games he downloaded left a virus behind. Nearly lost his dad a bushel of important business files, and it cost his old man a full week's pay to get the files decrypted. One of those hacking scams where they mutilate your files and then charge you to debug everything. How they snuck through his system he was still trying to figure out."

Expressions of disgust and exasperation all around.

"Despite these seemingly mild setbacks, the house was a major success, bringing Paul a promotion at work much to the congratulations of his co–workers, so when he came home that day, he decided to treat his wife to a date night, just the two of them. Jimmy was old enough to stay home alone, and the house would look after him. So, with a reminder for the teen not to go into the cerebrum of the house, Paul and Dorine left their son to his own devices. Jimmy did his homework and his chores and cleaned up around the house like he was expected to, but when the sun went down and still his parents hadn't returned, he began to grow bored. That's when it happened."

"When what happened?"

Lily pitches her voice, purposely amping up the brightness of the neural lights in her eyes.

"'How can I keep you occupied, young master?'"

Javier shivers as Lily dims the accoutrements.

"That night, all alone, while his parents drank and ate and celebrated, the house spoke to Jimmy for the first time. He couldn't for the life of him remember if he'd ever heard the house speak to anyone. An A.I. perhaps? Curious, Jimmy went to investigate himself, sneaking down to his father's office to check the main hub and found the door ajar, a neon green glow emanating from within. 'Come on in, young master,' the A.I. said again, and just before Jimmy could respond, his parents arrived home.

"Jimmy told his father about what happened, and in a panic, the man disappeared into the hub to sort out the mysterious voice. He didn't surface again until the next day when Jimmy heard a loud shout.

"He rushed into the office to find his father on the floor with vines growing from his augmentations. They were everywhere, growing from his mechanical limb, from his cranial disks and neural nodes, even growing from the dental caps inside his mouth.

"'Ca–call your mother,' his father choked out, and Jimmy was quick to listen. His mom helped his dad to the car, taking him to the hospital, but before he left, his dad told him in no uncertain terms. 'Stay out of the office!'

"And so, they left, leaving Jimmy home alone. The hours passed, the clock tick, tick, ticking down the seconds, the minutes, the hours until..."

Lily lowers her voice again, this time to a husky, seductive timbre, and beside her, Sebastian, color seeping into his cheeks, unzips the top of his coat.

"'Jimmy,' a voice whispered through the comm system. '*Jimmy.*' It was the same voice that spoke to him the night before only this time it seemed more... other, more mystic, more alluring. '*Come play with me, Jimmy.*' And Jimmy, helpless to resist the enchanting voice, snuck down to his dad's computer where the voice beckoned to him. A phantom hand gestured to him."

Lily lifts a hand making a "come hither" motion with her fingers to Sebastian, who leans closer in response.

"He crept down the stairs. Pit pat, pit pat, pit pat. To the state–of–the–art computer on the brand new, redwood desk. The door to the office stood ajar, a dull green glow emanating from its confines. Just like the night before, but this time, there were no interruptions. So, Jimmy tip–toed his way forward, put his hand on the doorknob, pulled it open, and—"

"BOO!"

Jeanine screams as Kyle glomps her from behind. Javier's mug flies through the air, and Derrick falls off his seat.

"Kyle, you jerk!"

Kyle laughs like an asthmatic hyena, doubled over and kekaw–ing as Javier dabs, crestfallen, at the cocoa now spilled down his coat.

"You bunch of noodles! I can't believe I got you so good."

"Way to interrupt just as the story was getting to the scary part." Jeanine shoves Kyle away.

"I am the scary part, sweet stuff."

Kyle pops the cap off a beer bottle taken from KC's back. The drone gives a little brreeep when the man gives her a little stroke on the head.

"Clearly." Jeanine rolls her eyes. "Finish the story, Lil. What happened to Jimmy after he opened the door?"

"No one knows."

"What?"

"No one knows what happened to Jimmy. When his parents got home, he was nowhere to be found. They searched everywhere. His bedroom, the kitchen, the attic, even the basement. It was like the kid just vanished into thin air. And when they checked the office, the computer was overgrown with moss and tree matter, like the desk had come alive again to grow around the technology. On the blinking screen was Jimmy's favorite computer game and a single flashing message.

"'Game Over.'"

Sebastian whistles.

"Jimmy Cartridge was never found, despite years of searching. In their grief, Paul and Dorine left the house where their son went missing, moving far away with their belongings. Naturally, Paul didn't leave the mainframe, setting up their system in a new smart house, and for a while everything was fine. Except, some days, when Jimmy's dad is working in his office at the hub, the last video game Jimmy ever played will open up on its own and an otherworldly voice will invite his dad to play."

Derrick shivers, culling the gooseflesh on his arms. "Oh lawd, that ending."

Jeanine, however, scoffs, shoving Kyle next to her.

"Too bad it didn't have the impact it would have if a certain somebody hadn't come barreling in in the middle of the story."

"So did the forest sprite merge with the computer?" asks Javier to Lily's responding shrug. "Creepy."

"That's why we teach the kiddos to stay as far away from magic as possible," says Sebastian. "You don't mix magic and technology, even accidentally. Too much bullshit might arise."

"Hn, sounds like a load of crock to me." laughs Kyle.

"Well, I liked it!" declares Jeanine. "Thanks for sharing, Lily."

"How's your ankle feeling, Javi?"

"The swelling's already diminished, and I think I can walk on it again. Should be good as new come morning."

Derrick runs a hand down his husband's back.

"Perhaps we should hit the sack. It's getting late, and we have even more trekking to do tomorrow."

IV

Rocky Horror Picture Show

"**I** CAN'T BELIEVE FUMIKO—SENSEI GAVE ME *an Inadequate on my last paper.*"

"*Here, let me see.*"

Wren pulls Lily's holo over to her. She has her stylus between her teeth and a paper textbook in her lap. The other girl has been working quietly on her latest punishment paper. How she hasn't managed to get herself dismissed is beyond Lily, but she guesses if anyone knows how to write a perfect paper for Fumiko Miyazaki, it would be Wren Nocturne. The Queen of Extracurricular Assignments.

"*Well, here's your problem. You've gotten the laws of magic backwards. It isn't cause and effect. It's effect without cause. Witchcraft doesn't need an incentive, just an intention.*"

"*Yeah, I don't understand that. How can you have an effect without a cause?*"

"*Okay, think about it this way. How do you start a house fire?*"

Lily frowns. "I don't know. Light a match or a candle and forget it's lit, I guess."

"*Right, well a witch doesn't need the match or the candle. They just conjure the flame, and the house goes up in smoke.*"

"But isn't that the cause then? Magic caused the fire."

"According to Lockecraft's theory, a causality needs to be measurable by time, space, and mass. Magic isn't. It changes too much. It can shift between tangible and intangible. It can be here and there. It can be now and then. It can alter time, space, and mass at will, changing the history of an electron into something unrecognizable to our data systems."

"So, magic can't be a cause?"

"Not for our purposes, no. It's immeasurable. That's why when we look for evidence of magic, we don't look for the cause, we look for the absence of a cause. Don't look for the match or the candle. Look for the absence of either."

"Ugh! I think I'm getting a headache."

The other girl chuckles.

"I wouldn't think about it too much. Rhyme and reason are the least of arcane concern. Just check your theorems over; I'm sure you'll do better on the next paper." Wren looks at her sidelong. "Honestly though? It's all a load of crock. Any attempt to scientifically analyze magic is superfluous at best. If you want to understand something, you need to look at it from the perspective of the people who live with it, and technomancers don't live with witch magic."

Lily wakes with a start.

Wren Nocturne? She hasn't thought about Wren in years, at least not in a personal sense. Wren helped her with her schoolwork on more than a few occasions during the summit. Think quantum physics is harrowing on the brain? Try arcane physics. That's a whole 'nother ball game. Magic defies so much of what natural science establishes as law and order: witches defy gravity, lycans defy thermodynamics/conservation of mass, and vampyres... Well, vampyres defy a lot of things. Chemically, they're more closely related to a virus than a human. It's really no wonder magic and science found themselves on opposite sides of a war.

Sebastian is turned away from her, sleeping half on his stomach and half on his side, his hip nudged into her thigh.

He snores into his pillow, the little breathing strip on his nose doing absolutely nothing to assuage the sound other than making him look kind of cute. One of his students got him a pack of colorful strips as a teaching appreciation gift. It was supposed to be a gag gift since the kid's father was an old roommate of Sebastian's, but he kept them anyway, and tonight, he's sporting a pink strip with red polka dots.

Lily rolls to her other side, content to go back to sleep until her bladder makes itself known.

Oh, no. This is the dreaded moment. She needs to pee, and she is going to have to do it in the woods, in the middle of the night.

She lies on her back, exasperated and reluctant to acknowledge the cruel call of nature.

Damnit! Why couldn't they have just gone glamping like normal people? What are they? Heathens?! If there was ever proof evolution, industrialization, and innovation are moot endeavors, it is in the entire concept of camping trips. No one goes camping for real anymore, at least not sensible people, and bathrooms are a necessity, not a luxury.

She untangles herself from their double sleeping bag, careful not to let too much of their shared heat out, and crawls her way to the tent flap. The zipper is noisy compared to the chirps of crickets, but Sebastian doesn't stir, heavy sleeper he is. She's seen the man sleep through a hurricane, yet he always wakes when she is out of bed for too long.

Jeanine's tent is on the opposite side of the campfire from theirs. Javier and Derrick set theirs up a ways away for a bit of privacy, and Kyle's tent, a commando–style affair, lightweight and easy to hike with, is pitched between two trees across the clearing, KC sleeping in front. The little bot's light system broadcasts its snooze cycle via a steady pulsing wavelength, visually akin to a snore. The perfect location for a night sentry to position. Kyle may be a lot of things, but he and Sebastian were Eagle Scouts once upon a time. He knows his camping stuff.

The fire has long since burned down. Nothing but embers glow in the pit. It still holds a bit of warmth, though not nearly enough to stave off the chill of the night. Goosebumps prickle along her arms and legs, her pajamas too thin. She should have packed her flannels. Sebastian told her as much, but she was under the impression they would be camping somewhere in Aighneas, not somewhere just south of the damned pole.

Oh, she is not looking forward to having to pee in the open air. Thank goodness Javier and Derrick had the good sense to bring toilet paper. It's even biodegradable.

Holding her prize, the roll of paper fished out of Derrick's knapsack, to her chest inside her coat, she hurries her way into the trees until she feels she is a decent distance from the rest of camp. She turns back to look, and while she can see the glow of their nightsticks, she can't actually see their tents, which is exactly her goal. She'll see one of her companions coming her way before they see her; therefore, no unexpected visitors.

She takes a moment to orient herself, setting the toilet paper on a branch and picking a spot that doesn't have poison ivy growing anywhere. As she is organizing her clothing, the hair at the nape of her neck prickles.

She turns about to check if anyone is coming, but there's no one around. The grasshoppers sing in the starlight, and the wind rustles gently through the trees, a nocturnal symphony surrounding her punctuated by the hoot of an owl. Lily has never been afraid of the dark, and she's too old to believe in spooky campfire stories. So why does she have this creeping sensation she is being watched?

She shakes her head and takes care of her business, cleaning up as best as she can considering there isn't exactly a bathroom she can use. As much as she loves Sebastian, he is sadly mistaken to think just because she has a military background means she'll relish the opportunity to pee in a bush, but she can make do. No point complaining about it.

"Bbrrr." She shivers, stomping her feet and reorienting herself toward their camp when a rustling sound to her left draws her attention. She pauses at the sound of leaves crunching underfoot. And the sense of being watched intensifies.

Even with her enhanced vision, Lily can't see very well in the dark. Not directly anyway. She looks down, peering the direction of the noise out of the corner of her eye. Just beyond her little potty spot is a thick–trunked maple surrounded by slimmer evergreens. The leaves are thinning out from shifting seasons, the chill of the air clinging to the boughs of the tree in the tiniest of icicles even though the autumnal equinox is but two weeks come and gone. (What is the temperature, anyway? 35 degrees according to her system monitor. No wonder she thought she was going to freeze her butt off.) There is a patch of darkness between the branches, thicker yet more finite than the surrounding blackness. She squints at it, leaning forward and trying to decide if her mind is playing tricks on her. Maybe she should have gotten that nightvision modification after all. Or a more powerful flashlight in her utility kit, the one she has already provides barely more light than a glow stick and doesn't reach much farther than a radius of two feet around her.

Just as she is about to chalk it up to her overactive imagination, the patch of darkness shifts.

Is there an animal sitting in the tree? There must be. Probably a bird or a wild cat resting in the trees after its midnight hunt, but she can't quite make it out. Cats are certainly known to stare, and nighttime predators require an acute sense of sight. How else do you expect to catch a mouse on a moonless night? Not that those happen much in Deus, but Dei does go dark every so often, and once Koi reaches his new moon phase, he'll seem to disappear from the sky entirely for almost three weeks before the first slivers of the greater moon return. So just because she can't see the animal doesn't mean it can't see her.

She takes a step forward, leaning against a nearby tree as she goes up on her toes, trying to catch a glimpse of the creature in the tree.

A shriek rings in the distance, and Lily whirls around so fast, a tree branch whips her across the face, stinging something fierce along her left cheek, and when she touches the spot, her fingers come away damp.

Leaves crunch behind her.

She pivots, slipping on dew–slick grass. Her feet fly out from under her, the beam of her utility light going wide as a human foot disappears into the darkness followed by a long cow–like tail. Her scream, short but pitched, echoes through her whole body as she lands.

"Lily!"

It's Sebastian. The stars above her spin in a slow, blurry rotation. When she looks back to where she saw the flash of pale skin, there's nothing there.

"I'm here," she calls back, rolling onto her hands and knees. Ah, wire–cutters! Now she's covered in mud. At least she didn't land in the spot where she peed earlier. Then she would be covered in mud and her own piss.

"Are you alright?"

She makes her way to standing, trying in vain to pat the mud out of her pajama pants.

"I'm fine. Just—" A light shines in her face as Sebastian appears before her. "Just dirty."

He stifles a laugh with his fist.

She pouts.

"It's not funny, Sebastian!" she growls, shaking out her hair. Sprockets! She has twigs in her hair. Sebastian laughs harder. *Okay, maybe it is kind of funny...* She smacks him anyway. At least, he helps her pull the brambles out of her hair as he chortles.

"What were you doing out here?"

"I needed to pee, alright, and I tripped. Now my clothes are wet and muddy, I'm cold, and my boyfriend is laughing at me."

"I'm sorry, babe. You just look... Nevermind. You can borrow my clothes, unless of course you just want to sleep naked."

She can't see it in the dark, but she imagines his eyebrow is waggling.

"In your dreams, fly boy."

"Well, come back to bed so I can witness the most ethereal of sights as float off to slumberland."

She smacks him again. "Flirt."

"It's not flirting if I'm being honest. Oh, baby—" His tone changes from lighthearted and teasing to instantly concerned. "You're bleeding."

He touches her cheek, and the sting reminds her why she fell in the first place.

"Something startled me, and I cut my cheek on a branch."

"Glad I packed an old–fashioned first aid kit then. Come on. Let's get you cleaned up."

"Don't you want to check out what it was?"

"It was probably just an animal, Lil. Nothing to get uppity about. Come on. You're shivering. Let's get you back in the tent."

Sebastian takes her under his arm and escorts her back to camp. He bandages her cheek, helps her out of her soiled clothes, and tucks her up against him in their sleeping bag. Despite her earlier quip, she forgoes clothing, draping herself in his skin instead. He fondles her breasts and tangles his fingers in the soft fuzz of her mound, dipping into her folds to circle her pearl. When he hardens behind her, she rolls him over and mounts him, spearing herself on his aching cock with a gasp.

She rides him to orgasm, and he tongues her open in turn. They catch their breath together, Lily's head pillowed on Sebastian's shoulder. Sebastian has a tattoo on his chest. It's been there since before they got together. A simple piece, it's just a unicorn's silhouette, no detailing, just a wash of rainbow colors, and as she traces her fingers over the tattoo, she forgets all about the too quiet night and the rustling of leaves in a windless wood. About muddied footsteps and moonless, starless skies.

She forgets that, as he was leading her back to the barely lit fire, Lily only looked back once. Just once to affirm to herself there was indeed nothing there despite the burn of inhuman eyes tingling up her back.

Poison Girl

Nine Years Ago – 22nd Day in the Month of Songs, 1861 A.P. – The 247th Technomancer Trials – Shinka Temple

"GEEZE, I THOUGHT BEING IN THE mountains for the trials would be more whimsical. But it just rains all the time."

Wren shakes her hair out, tucking her hands under her head as she lays back on the towel she's spread over the grass.

"I mean, it is almost the Month of Storms. Its name isn't exactly arbitrary."

Their group of girls is sitting in the grass by the rock garden during their lunch break. It's the first sunny afternoon in days, and pretty much all of the remaining trial participants are eager to get some sunshine. They found a good spot underneath one of the pine trees, and the shade is worth having to clear out all of the fallen cones.

"Still, I'm getting so pasty pale being here," says Wren, rubbing more tanning oil into her chest.

She's hardly what Lily would consider pale. The girl's olive skin–tone might be a few shades lighter than it was a few weeks ago, but it's nothing compared to Lily's porcelain pink. Lily sits between Wren and Rhiannon, hiding under a floppy sunning hat while they lie in their spaghetti strap tops and shorts in a patch of sunlight, while Lydia, Selene, and Heather sit on the opposite side of the picnic blanket where the most shade is. Maybe she should move over to them before she ends up looking more like strawberry milk. Wren and Rhiannon wanted to sunbathe, and while Lily normally sits with the pair, she can already feel herself burning despite the sunblock she rubbed into her skin. Her dermal augmentations may filter out a large percentage of the UV rays, but they won't keep her skin from becoming lobster chic.

"I miss the beach," sighs Wren, laying back in the grass. "The water would be perfect for surfing by now. The waves are always the tallest in the spring."

"No, thank you," says Lily. "I burn like a ripe tomato in the sun."

"That's why you make a handsome boy rub lotion on your back," teases Selene from her cushy spot in the shade. "So, you don't burn."

"It would take a battalion of boys to keep my skin from burning."

"Ew," icks Lydia. "Why would you give a testosterone hyped boy an excuse to touch you?"

"Oh, I don't think Lily would mind the attention of our testosterone laden counterparts." Rhiannon smirks from under her sunglasses, the older girl's tawny brown skin already darkening to a cool coffee tone in the sunlight. "Isn't that right, Lily?"

Beside her, Wren exhales loudly. "Here comes the boy-talk again..."

"I'm not the one who's boy crazy, Rih."

"Mhmm, I'm not the one who spent the night in Lionheart's room last night."

Lily hits Rhiannon, aghast.

"Jerk! I told you that in confidence."

"Lily! You didn't!" exclaims Heather, aiming an electric fan at her face. It buzzes loudly on its highest setting to keep her cool

The blonde nods. "I did."

"Well, how was it?"

"It was fine, I guess. I don't really have anything to compare it to. It was my first time so…"

Wren sits up. "What! Was he at least careful?"

Lily turns to Wren in shock.

"Yeah. I–I mean, he didn't hurt me."

"My first time was terrible," says Selene. "The guy didn't know what he was doing at all. Lionheart seems much more capable. Good for you, Lily."

Heather heaves a dramatic sigh.

"Oh, to be a lesbian and never have to suffer the ill–attentions of fumbling boys. You ever want a real orgasm, you let me know."

"Heather's a true ladykiller."

"What about you, Lydia? Have you ever, ya know?" asks Lily.

"No," says Lydia, the oldest of them at twenty–one. "I want to wait until marriage."

"Lydia has a partner back home," says Heather. "You told me you've been together for how long?"

"Since we were seventeen."

"Wow! Do you think they're the one?"

"I don't know. Mel is sweet, but with me doing the trials this year, who knows if it'll happen? If I graduate, I'll probably have to move somewhere else, and Mel is kind of focused on becoming a nurse which will take another four or five years of university."

"Maybe they'll move with you?"

"Maybe." Lydia shrugs. "What about you, Wren? Are any of the rumors true?"

Wren doesn't even open her eyes to answer. "No. I'm a virgin."

"No, you're not!"

"Yes, I am."

"But your brother punched Llywelyn in the face for saying you spent the night with him after the Apprentice Ball."

"*Che*! I wouldn't touch that *pendejo* with a 39–and–a–half–foot pole."

"So, you've really never—"

"Nope."

"But you're so popular?"

Wren laughs. "So? I'm supposed to sleep with someone just because they like me?" Heather looks away, cowed by the sarcasm in Wren's words.

"Are you waiting until marriage then?"

"Me? Don't be ridiculous, Lydia. I'm not marriage material. I pity any poor man or woman who would want me as a wife. Besides 'wife,' what a lackluster title... And the wedding vows! 'Til death do us part!' It's such a cliche, and no one actually means it anymore. The whole ceremony is just the start of an overdone stage play." Wren sits up, clears her throat, and begins to recite the traditional wedding vows in a nasally voice. "We gather here today to unite so–and–so and so–and–so in, ehem..." she pinches her nose closed, "oily ma–tree–moan–ie."

The girls all burst out laughing. Lily laughs so hard, the water she was just drinking sprays out of her nose, inciting the other girls to laugh even harder. As she buries her face in napkins and towels, she notices Kaito Miyazaki glaring at them from the other side of the zen garden. She hiccups when she notices his sights are spinning, and he looks very much annoyed by their behavior. Outbursts of laughter probably aren't considered the most courteous of sounds in a zen garden.

"Guys!" she hisses, smacking the girls closest to her and gesturing toward the prince. Heather, Rhiannon, Lydia, and

Selene all pipe down, bowing their heads in deference to the prince, but Wren... Wren sits up taller and waves brightly at the stoic prince with her mechanical hand.

"Kaito–kun! Why don't you come join us? I packed some extra strawberries!"

The man's silvery gaze narrows at the girl. (It's so creepy how colorless his eyes are. She's never seen anyone with eyes like that.) How Wren doesn't just shrivel up like a raisin is far beyond Lily—that glare is so poisonous—but then he gets up and strides away without saying a word.

Wren cups her hands around her mouth and shouts at his retreating back. "If you change your mind."

The man gives her an annoyed harrumph and keeps walking, pointedly ignoring the Derivan girl, who merely giggles into her palm in response.

"Wren!" Lily proclaims, smacking the island girl in the shoulder.

"So scary!" shivers Lydia.

"Oh, please. He is so...Ah, I can't even!"

Wren flops backward on the grass in a huff.

"Speaking of handsome men..." Heather hides her face behind her palm, girlish and pink–faced.

"Oh hush! Prince Kaito doesn't pay much mind to anyone except Lady Wren."

"Oh, please." The girl shakes her fingers at Rhiannon. "If by 'pay much mind to' you mean glare at me and then storm away *con un palo nuevo en el culo*, you're correct. The guy hates my guts."

"If you're so sure he hates you, why are you always bothering him?"

Wren shrugs.

"He makes cute faces when he's angry."

Selene leans forward, a teasing smile on her face.

"I think you like him."

"Yes, because I so thoroughly enjoy having holes glared into my head."

"Maybe he'll bring you flowers one of these days." Rhiannon twirls a tiny grass flower between her fingertips. "Roses are so romantic. Or maybe he'll bring you cherry blossoms. They're so pretty!"

Wren wrinkles her nose. "Eh, roses are overrated, and pink is not really my favorite color."

"Oh, and what kind of flowers would impress the illustrious Wren Nocturne?"

"My favorite are amethyst saltwater lilies. They are the most gorgeous shade of purple with blue centers. They grow in the shallows offshore at home, and at night when they bloom, they glow this really pretty blue–green color."

Rhiannon pulls up a picture of one on her comm unit, and Lily leans over to take a look at the pretty purple flower, opened up with dozens of pointed petals and framed by lily pads.

"Saltwater lilies. I mean they're pretty, but aren't they poisonous?"

"Exactly," says Wren, matter–of–factly. "Just like love. Beautiful but dangerous. My mother once read me a fairy tale about a sea nymph born from a lily. She fell in love with a handsome prince who in turn married her to save her from a witch's curse."

"Aww, that's so romantic."

"Not really. The prince lived far away from the sea, and without the freedom of the open water, the nymph withered away into nothing."

"That's awful! Why would you like a flower with a story like that linked to it?"

"It's just a story, Selene. It's not really true. Besides, the saltwater lily symbolizes love without chains or restrictions. Isn't that the way true love should be? Undefined by traditional boundaries and conventions."

While the other girls coo in agreement, Lily can't help but disagree. She's the kind of girl who reads fashion magazines and watches wedding reality shows. She imagines what her gown will look like, what her groom will say, the kind of flowers she'll have, the kind of life she'll have with him afterward, the children they'll raise.

She doesn't say anything then, but later that evening, when she is hanging out in Wren's dorm, she asks.

"But wouldn't you want to be with the person you love? That's what marriage is. The promise you'll be with someone always."

"Choosing to love someone and be with them is one thing. But marriage is a completely different thing, not always synonymous with love, unfortunately. The only reason I'm here is because my stepmother wants me to 'inspire a favorable match.' But I'll show her. When I go home as a technomancer, her dreams of selling me to the highest bidder will be sand in the sea."

"But what if you fell in love with someone? Wouldn't you want to be with them? Wouldn't you want them to be with you?"

"Not if it meant they would have to give up the things most important to them. As romantic as the notion of 'all you need is love' is, it's unrealistic. People need friends, family, their careers, their hobbies. No one person can make up for having to give up the most important things. That leads to resentment, and no relationship can survive true resentment. I would rather be apart from someone than force them into a life that may not make them happy."

VI

Radio Static

Present – 31st Day in the Month of Darkness 1870 A.P. – Hexennacht – Unknown Location

"Who the fuck took my axe?"

"No one took your axe, Kyle."

It's too early for this. The sun hasn't even risen yet and already there is yelling outside. Lily stretches out, still naked between the soft downy of the sleeping bags. Sebastian is gone. Up already, dealing with his brother.

"Then where is my fucking axe?"

Lily rolls her eyes and pulls on her pants. With a slide of the zipper, she slides herself into the dewy morning light, the smallest of icicles melting with the sunrise.

"Hey, Lily, you want some eggs?"

Derrick, wielding a cast iron skillet, hovers over a gently burning fire pit. He's fed some twigs and dried up leaves into the flame to make it just hot enough to cook over.

"You brought eggs."

"Powdered but I know the value of good spices. There's bacon, too, and I think Javier packed some energy bars."

Lily helps herself to a few strips of crispy bacon. It's a little blacker than she would like, but it's good and the crunch distracts from the argument still unfolding across the camp. Sebastian and his brother go back and forth, back and forth in their home language. Something Germanic spoken in the smaller countries between Seraphim and Aighneas. Sebastian once took Lily to visit his mom in New Jutland. She lived in one of those assisted living communities. All the old ladies spoke in this sweet dialect that made them sound like the kind of women who once traded stories around the dairy farm while milking the cows.

"Anybody know what they're saying?"

"No clue," answers Jeanine. "I only speak common."

Javier shrugs. "I know a bit of Hexen, which sounds similar, but I haven't a clue what they're saying."

"That's because Hexen is about as different from the Germanic languages as Hanasu is from Japanese or Derivan from Spanish. Similar enough to be recognizable but too far removed to provide any kind of true cross–fluency."

Lily is taking another bite of bacon when a pair of familiar hands clamp down on her shoulders.

"Happy Halloween!!"

She jumps. "Sebastian! You scared me."

"Well, 'tis the season for a good fright."

Kyle traipses over and abruptly stamps out the tiny fire. "Alright, banquet hall is closed. Pack up your shit and let's get going."

Derrick and Javier scramble to salvage the pots and pans from the man's boot while Jeanine tries to save the food from flying ash.

"Hey, what the hell, man?"

"I said we're going."

"Hey, take it easy. None of us took your damn axe."

Kyle huffs, then smiles his winning smile.

"I know. Sorry. It's just we're burning daylight, and we still have a ways to go before we get to the spot. If we don't get going, it'll be pitch black by the time we get there. Not exactly primetime for a photo op. I just—" He cuts himself off and threads flesh fingers through his hair. "I just want to make sure you all have a good time. It's Halloween after all. Hexennacht! The best holiday of the year. Let's not waste it over some over–salted eggs."

Derrick lifts a hand to his chest, aghast.

"They are perfectly salted, thank you very much, and you certainly had no problem scarfing them down a minute ago."

"They were over–salted," coos Javier.

Derrick harrumphs at his husband even as the smaller man tries to smooch a kiss onto the side of his face.

And just like that, the tension evaporates.

As she is helping Sebastian pack up their tent, Lily can't help but glance toward the poor splintered tree Kyle chopped up last night. A deep fissure, like a jagged scar cracked through the center of the poor maple, is the only remaining evidence of the axe previously embedded in the trunk. The wound is deep enough for Lily to fit her whole hand inside. It would've taken some serious muscle to pull that axe loose, and Derrick is the only unaugmented person in their group who could possibly manage it. Lily doesn't have the augmentations necessary for abnormal strength.

So, who took the axe? Or better yet: *what* took the axe?

They trek through the woods, Kyle forging his way forward despite his lack of wood–rending equipment. Javier, trudging along at the rear, stumbles for the nth time in as many minutes.

"Hey, Kyle, how much farther? I think the girls are getting tired."

Jeanine scoffs. "Speak for your own asthmatic self, Javi."

"I haven't had asthma since I was a teenager."

And as though to contradict himself, he coughs. A nice, long hacking fit that inspires Derrick to pull out his husband's inhaler.

"Mhmm, in the words of William Golding, 'Sucks to your Assmar!'"

Javier pouts at the proffered medicine but takes a big puff, scowling at his sister the whole time.

"Don't worry, scrawny legs," Kyle calls back over his shoulder. "We're almost there."

"And where is there?" asks Lily, side–eyeing her boyfriend. "Some great rock formation? An actual glamping site in the middle of nowhere with running water? Or is it just an empty clearing in the middle of the forest carved out by aliens? Huh! Sebastian, did you bring me here to abduct me? Are you taking me to your mothership and never taking me back home?"

Sebastian laughs, snaking an arm around her waist.

"You'll see. Don't worry. You'll love it!"

"I better love it, or you're going to be sleeping outside the tent tonight."

"I submit myself to your judgement, milady." He leans toward her face, but just as she closes her eyes, something scurries past her feet with a yowl. Startled, she jumps, her head slamming into Sebastian's chin. His teeth clank together, and he grabs for her arm as he careens to the side. They slam into a nearby tree as a fluffy, ringed tail disappears into the underbrush.

"Ow…"

She has a goose egg already forming on the top of her head, and Sebastian clutches at his chin, a thin line of blood trailing from his lip.

"Ah, fuck."

"Did you bite your lip?"

He spits some blood out of his mouth. "My tongue, yeah."

"Hey, you two okay?"

Kyle doubled back to check on them.

"Just an animal," Sebastian answers, rubbing the bruise already forming on his jaw. "Startled us."

"Did you see what it was?"

"A raccoon, I think. Didn't get a good look at it."

Kyle hums. "Well, hurry up. We're here."

He then walks off, leaving the couple behind.

"Your head okay?"

With an ache already swelling behind her eyes, Lily checks in with her internal systems to see if she has a concussion, but her vital signs read normal. Just a headache, then. Damn, Sebastian has a chin sharp enough to cut glass.

"Yeah, it's fine. I'm sorry you bit your tongue."

"Eh, it's just a tongue, but unfortunately that means tonight I won't be able to, you know..."

Oh, she's gonna smack that shit–eating grin off his face! "Perv."

"You love it."

"Fortunately, for you. Otherwise, I'd have to find a replacement for my injured boyfriend. Oh, wait, nevermind. I did pack my bullet. Guess you're off duty, buddy."

"I'll show you 'off duty.'"

He lunges for a retaliatory tickle. She squeals, dodging around waggling fingers, and races after their friends. The wind tousles her hair, the smell of the forest rich as she sprints through the trees, leaves crunching under her feet and the air cool in her lungs.

"You can't escape me."

Laughter, deep and rich and far too happy to be menacing.

"Mhmm, just try to catch me, big boy."

She's faster than him, naturally. Her augmentations make it so she can run faster, harder, longer than any normal, but she isn't pushing herself. She isn't really even trying to get away. She wants to be caught. That primitive adrenaline of being hunted by a hunter you wouldn't mind being eaten by. Little Red Riding Hood and the Big Bad Wolf, a roleplay in the woods. Too bad her wolf now has an injured tongue.

Broad hands dig into her hips, knobbing around the bones of her pelvis and spinning her. Her backpack gets squished against a tree, her fingers winding around his neck. His face is wind–burned and pink, his breath puffing in short bursts of steam between them, and she leans up to steal the breath from his lips.

He tastes like toothpaste and the instant coffee he drank this morning, fresh but strong. Like a peppermint cappuccino even though pumpkin spice is all the rage this time of year. If she were home, she would have baked a jack–o–lantern pie: pumpkin puree, whipped together with spices, then spread through a pie crust. She likes to add a lattice of crust over the top in the shape of a toothy pumpkin face and bake it for about twenty minutes.

She wonders what the neighborhood children will dress up as this year. There will be the usual ghosts and witches and vampires, probably a few kiddos here and there dressed as their favorite hexen–slaying technomancer. Last year, a number of little girls dressed up as Morrigan Gewalt, the president of Aighneas and the current primarch of the technomancer council. Even a few boys dressed up as the fearsome woman known as The Morrigan. Lots of kids loved dressing up as the Murasakan technomancers—their garb is just so unique compared to everyone else.

Lily had been planning to dress up as a fairy this year, something sweet and innocent so as not to scare the kids, even if Sebastian had been planning on going as a zombie or something equally undead. But then they decided on this camping trip. She meant to bring a mask with her for posterity's sake but forgot in the flurry of trying to pack the car.

Sebastian's mouth moves over hers, and unthinking, she presses forward with her tongue. The coppery tang of blood meets her taste buds. She jerks backward as he hisses.

"Oops! I forgot."

"You know for having a computer in your head, your memory sucks."

"It's not like I can make a neural checklist of every little thing."

"Even so—"

"Hey, Lily, you have to see this!"

Javier's call of her name draws her attention, and she slides around Sebastian and hurries along, stopping just short of running into Derrick's broad back.

"Whoa."

The clearing they've entered is anything but empty. The ruins of an old cottage rest on the far side of the clearing just inside the tree line. Neglect leaving it in disrepair, ivy grows up the side, one of the windows hangs off its hinges, the door is cracked down the center, and leaves and dirt trail into the small home. She can even see the branches of a tree poking through the roof just past the crumbling chimney. There is a weed–infested garden, an abandoned tricycle, a deflated flat ball, and a rotting structure that looks like it might have once been a cat's climbing house.

All these things on their own are relatively benign. Homes are abandoned all the time, especially in a place as isolated as this. And there are no signs of death anywhere, no rancid scents, no flies, no bodies frozen in the ground. There's absolutely no reason for this place to put her on edge, so why does she feel like an intruder in a very private place?

Haunted...

This is a place where people once laughed and played and lived. Now left desolate, Time and Decay are the only residents here.

The aura of magic she has felt in the whole of the forest is heavier here. The kind of imprint left on a place that has been hearth and home to magic for a long time.

This is where Sebastian wanted to bring her? To an abandoned house in an enchanted forest for Hexennacht? It's romantic, she guesses, if she believed in that kind of thing. But why? When she turns to him in question, he just beams at her, proud for some unfathomable reason. She is clearly missing something.

"How is this place still standing?" asks Jeanine, striding toward the ruined home.

"Jeanine!" scolds Lily.

"What? It's just an old house. I want to see what's inside."

"Said the protagonist of every horror movie ever."

"Shut up, Derrick."

"I'm just saying this is the part where somebody either goes missing or the first body is found."

Kyle gives an uncharacteristic snicker.

Jeanine shoulders her way through the crooked door, flinching when dust and debris fall from the ceiling but then striding right on through into the dark confines of the cottage.

"Jeanine," growls Lily, trailing after the younger woman.

The inside of the house is as dilapidated as the outside and twice as disconcerting. In a dusty kitchenette, there's an overhead rack where the stringy remains of once carefully tended herbs hang limp and black, weeping from lack of care. There are pots and pans, tarnished with rust and crawling with insects on the stove. Was someone cooking when the calamity struck? But when she looks in the pots, there is no food, just a gelatinous fluid being feasted on by centipedes. Over the oven rests a wood–carved wheel with seasonal etchings decorating each notch.

Across from the kitchenette is a living space with a gnarled rug settled in the center, a rocking chair, and cushioned sofa. The cushions have been long ravaged by animals, tears and holes scratched into the fabric and the stuffing scattered on the ground. A bookcase stands mysteriously devoid of books, one of the shelves torn from its place. In echo to the tricycle outside, there are toys strewn about the floor: a set of soft building blocks, stuffed animals with patchy spots of faux fur and unravelling seams, a pair of pink child–sized slippers.

Most disconcerting though is the cauldron broken on its side in the fireplace and shattered crystals on the floor.

"This is a witch's cottage."

And witches mean ghosts.

"We shouldn't be in here—"

"Whoa…"

Jeanine's awestruck exclamation draws Lily's attention.

"Jeanine, I said not to touch anything!" she says, taking a wad of papers from the younger woman.

"They're just drawings."

Jeanine has dug around in one of the dresser drawers and unearthed what is indeed a collection of drawings stacked together haphazardly.

Lily leafs through the pictures, the crayon masterpieces of a toddler. There's a rough sketch of a cat, notable only by the whiskers, pointed ears, and a triangular pink nose, and two four–legged blobs, denoted as dogs by the scrawled "BARK" next to their noses. There are stick–like figures of people. Two women: one dark–skinned and tall holding a broomstick and the other yellow–haired and sitting by a tree, a tail waving behind her from under her dress. Pictures of butterflies and animals and another black–haired, green–eyed woman with music notes dancing around her head. Some of the drawings are even colored across composition paper, over musical scores handwritten by an adult hand.

"Eep!"

A noisy clatter followed by the shattering of glass. Lily looks up to see Jeanine sheepishly holding a now broken mirror, etched through with strange sigils and shapes, including a five–pointed star now cracked down the center and missing one and a half of its points. Lily doesn't like the look of the designs, but she doesn't remember enough from her arcane alphabet classes to know what they might signify.

"Really?"

"Sorry," replies Jeanine, dropping the cracked mirror on a moth–eaten sofa. "Guess that's seven years of bad luck for me."

The joke isn't funny. Not here. And Jeanine's wide grin just makes it worse.

"Please, don't touch anything."

"Aye, aye, captain!"

As Jeanine wanders into the back part of the house, Lily turns her attention back to the pictures in her hand.

There is a boxy figure of a man, tall next to a small child, with two sticks poking from his back. Next to the man's figure in purple crayon is written "TekNo MaAn." There are a few pictures of "tekno maan," one featuring him with the singing woman, another with the child in–between, the man and the singing woman holding onto either hand. But the last drawing... The last drawing in the stack gives her pause.

It's the singing woman by herself, the child's attempt to draw a portrait of her face. Bright–green eyes, dark curly hair, and pink lips drawn into a crooked smile. At her brow, in bright green crayon, three interlocking spirals sit, and it is this detail that makes Lily's fingers go numb, especially when considering at the corner of the page the word "MaMa" is written.

"You've got to be kidding me."

"Lily?"

Lily storms from the house, the pictures gripped tight in her fist as she makes her way toward Sebastian. He and Javier have their heads tucked together in a most conspiratorial way, and it only riles Lily's anger.

"Sebastian, you are going to tell me right now. Which forest are we in?"

"Whoa, Lily, hold on. I told you. This is Blackwood Forest. This is all part of the trip. Kyle mapped this all out for us."

"This is not Blackwood Forest, and I don't care if this is part of the trip or not. Now, you tell me where we are."

"Lily, calm down. What does it matter which forest we're in? It's just a forest. Kyle wouldn't have brought us here if it wasn't safe."

"Do you even realize whose house this is?"

Sebastian blinks owlishly at the building. "No. Am I supposed to?"

"That house belonged to the Songstress of Lorelei."

Sebastian turns to look at his brother. "What?"

"This is Lorelei Forest," says Kyle.

"What did you say?" squeaks Derrick.

"Lorelei Forest. You know, the haunted forest where the Songstress of Lorelei supposedly bit the bullet."

Javier and Derrick make a startled sound behind them, and Lily rounds on her boyfriend.

"Did you know about this!?"

"Lily, don't be mad at Bassy," calls Kyle. "He didn't know. I showed him the map but not the actual names of anything."

"You told me," says Sebastian, "this was an unexplored part of Blackwood."

"I lied because I didn't want to freak anyone out before we got here."

"You kept this a secret!" she shouts, rounding on the older man. Sebastian holds her back. "You brought us into a cursed forest, and you kept it a secret!"

"It's not cursed," Kyle spits back. "You said so yourself. It's just hexen tales."

"This is where she died! And you think—" A sob chokes its way out of Lily's throat. Sebastian folds her into his chest.

"Kyle, what the hell were you thinking bringing us here?"

His chest rumbles under her ear.

"You were the one talking about wanting to do something big for your girlfriend this weekend, and you mentioned she was into hexen shit, and my boss mentioned wanting to look to open up tours here, so I figured, hey! Why don't I bring my little bro, his girlfriend, and a couple of her friends to check out the tour? Depending on what you guys think, I'll be able to start booking people as early as next week."

"Wait a minute," says Javier. "Let me get this straight. You are planning to take money from people so you can lead them into the very forest where the Songstress of Lorelei killed herself."

"Why not? People love ghost tours, and who wouldn't want the chance to see the ghost of the Songstress of Lorelei? It's an untapped gold mine. And once we find the actual grounds where she kicked it—"

Lily rips her face out of Sebastian's shirt.

"We are not looking for the place where Wren Nocturne died!" shouts Lily. "Wren was—"

Wren was my friend! Lily nearly shouts it but bites her tongue before the words can leave her mouth.

"Look, Lily," says Kyle, putting on a charming smile nearly identical to his brother's. It looks wrong on his face. "I know you're upset, but I swear to you, I scouted this place out weeks ago. There aren't any real ghosts around here, at least not any hexen ghosts, so there isn't anything that will hurt us around here, and the Songstress hasn't so much as made a peep since her death. Bassy told me you were doing your research on her, so I thought you'd like it."

"You thought I would want to see the place where a woman was driven so mad by magic, she ended her own life."

"Okay, okay. You're the boss. We don't have to go to that spot."

Jeanine steps forward, a plying look on her face.

"Lily, your thesis is literally about the Songstress of Lorelei. Wouldn't it be cool to actually stay and investigate the last known place where she lived? The ghost story is just an added bonus."

She can't be serious. She wants to stay here. Lily can see it in her pleading expression. Disbelief, cold and cloying, rocks through her as she recognizes the same exact look on Javier, Derrick, and even Sebastian's face.

"You want to stay here."

"It's just a ghost story, Lily," says Javier, sinking into his hip.

"Ghost stories aren't just games around a campfire, Javi. They exist for a reason."

"We know that, but you heard my brother," Sebastian implores her. "Kyle says this place is perfectly safe. He's scouted the whole area."

"At night, too," adds Kyle.

"See, at night, as well, and nothing happened."

"Not on Hexennacht!"

He holds her by the upper arms, and god, he's lucky he's handsome; otherwise, she would be punching his nose in.

"Lily, baby, I understand you're scared—"

"I'm not scared."

"—but nothing is going to happen."

"We're too far in to make it back out before dark, anyway," says Kyle.

"Why don't we go ahead and set up camp?" provides Javier, looking at Derrick.

"Oh, maybe I can get the oven inside the house to work. I can cook a real spread for dinner."

Javier's eyes brighten, turning to Lily. "We can explore the surrounding area. You can take pictures, and then when you present your dissertation, you'll have awesome photographs no one has ever seen before. Hell, we can even sleep inside the house. Nothing like having a real roof overhead."

"No one is sleeping inside!"

No one would be setting foot inside of that house. Not if she can help it.

"And no pictures either."

Let the ghosts of the past rest in peace.

"Okay, shit, Lily. If I'd known you'd be a total bitch about this, I'd—"

Sebastian angles himself toward his brother. "Kyle, shut up."

Lily yanks herself from Sebastian's arms and runs, deaf to the panicked shouts of her name. Tears blur her eyes, she is so, so angry at all of them.

VII

Fairy Dance

SHE RUNS FOR WHAT FEELS LIKE HOURS BUT is really probably just five or ten minutes. She can't hear anyone coming after her, but she can't hear much of anything right now anyway, the blood pounding in her ears, and she pays so little attention to her surroundings, it's a wonder she doesn't stumble her way into a ravine or river.

Shortness of breath forces an end to her run to nowhere. She pants, hands on her knees and a stitch in her side, trying to catch her breath. Curse her sorry lungs! She used to be able to run for hours on end. Now, in the wave of anxiety–driven adrenaline, her own body fights against itself, a constant push and pull between the tech systems that keep her alive and an overactive immune system that doesn't recognize the difference between her own tissue and foreign invaders.

Counting through her breath cycles, her heart slowly returns to a reasonable beat, her muscles unclench, and her tech system whirrs to life, filtering out the excess CO_2 and flooding oxygen into her muscles before her system attacks itself. When her lungs fall in line once again, she lifts her head and takes a look around for the first time since she started running.

Kyle was right when he said it was getting too late to make it back out of the woods. The watercolor wash of sunset skirts over the treetops, reflecting a crystal–clear amethyst in an unending expanse of perfect glossy silver.

She's found a lake.

The water reflects the sky as clearly as mirror glass, unbroken and undisturbed, as pure as the legendary sword Excalibur given to King Arthur by The Lady of the Lake. When she was studying in the Abbey, the congressional capital of Aighneas, she took a course on old world literature, some of the texts dating back as far as 2200 B.C. While Earthling humans believed the legends to be no more than myths, their ancestors, the pagans who forged Deus, knew better. See, the legend, as written by a human man, is a twisted rendition of the truth. Excalibur, having been the athame of the Lady of the Lake, was stolen from her by Arthur to devastating effect. It was another witch, Merlin, who took the blade back and returned it to its rightful owner. It came over with the witches when the gods carved out Deus for them. Rumor has it the king's blade is currently hidden in a vault deep under the ocean with a host of other powerful athames protected by the merfolk and only accessible to witches of the sovereign bloodline.

A fish breaks the surface to gobble up an insect, the splash so noisy in relation to the previous unbroken stillness that it echoes through the entire clearing. Ripples lap at the pebbles scattered along the shoreline, the watercress wave under the surface, and at the disturbance, a sparkle of fireflies take flight. They dance and flit along the shore, weaving in and out of the trees, getting bigger and brighter the closer they get to her until she realizes they're not fireflies at all.

They're fairies.

Real, glitter–dusting fairies, no bigger than the length of her pinkie. They waltz around the area in duets and trios, flickering and fluttering through different colors in a sparkling kaleidoscope. It's like sitting at the center of a living, breathing rainbow.

Such sights, as commonplace as they were before The Vanquishing, are rare these days. Magical beings of all kinds going into hiding—if they didn't die out completely—in the wake of an inordinate amount of magic being snuffed out in one fell swoop. It's cathartic, almost: knowing there are magics more powerful than science, and life's ability to persist is one of them. Thanos! The Vanquishing happened less than ten miles from this very spot, the city of Lorelei nothing but rubble where once was a neutral zone between hexen and human+.

How could she completely fail to realize which forest they were in? No wonder she flunked out of her technomancer trials.

"Hey."

Sebastian's voice carries across the clearing of fairies. The dancing fae scatter, flying upward in fright before descending back down as Sebastian approaches her. He's refreshed his cologne, the scent of sandalwood and leather embracing her cool and familiar. He's wearing Steel Noir, a scent Lionheart endorsed a few years back. As much as technomancers are warriors, some of them embrace the celebrity of being the elite of society. Selene has done quite a few modeling campaigns over the years, and Jamar even starred in a movie not too long ago, so can Lily really blame Lionheart for choosing to sit in on a commercial photoshoot or two? He's a handsome man, and with the current climate, technomancers aren't exactly racking in the paid missions. There aren't exactly enough hexen wreaking havoc to keep the technomancers busy.

Sebastian winds his arms around her, and Lily sinks into his embrace. His chin rests bony on her shoulder as he looks out over the water, more fairy lights blinking over the once again still surface. Even through the thick thermal coat she wears, she can feel his body heat. He's like a human furnace. In the summertime, she can barely stand cuddling for too long post-coitus—he runs so hot.

"I know you're mad at me, but I wanted to say I'm sorry. I didn't realize Kyle lied, and if I'd known the reason he chose this place, I would have told him to choose a different forest. I told him we wanted to go on a camping trip, not a ghost hunt."

Her shoulders sag.

"I'm not mad. I'm just frustrated. You guys don't understand, and I just... nevermind."

"Tell me. I want to understand."

"I knew her, Sebastian. I knew Wren. She was... She was my classmate at the summit. She helped me on my assignments. Before Wren was the Songstress of Lorelei, she was a brilliant technomancer, and she... she was someone I would have called a friend."

"Oh, baby. I didn't know."

"I know you didn't know. I didn't tell you, and it's not exactly something any of us who knew her ever actually talk about. Heck, not even her own brother will say her name anymore. If it weren't for family records, you would forget the Vulcan of Deriva even had a half-sister."

Because that's what people do when they want to forget all about something. They shove it in the darkest corners of their closets, and they never mention it again, but if there was anyone who didn't deserve to be shoved in a box...

"Wren was the most bubbly, optimistic person I've ever met. She didn't take no for an answer and never let anything get her down. I–I don't understand how someone like that could take their own life."

"Hon, she went crazy. The reports said she suffered from magically induced psychosis. If she hadn't done it herself, the League would've had no choice but to put her down."

"Yeah, according to the League."

"What does that mean?" he asks, confused. Oh, she's put her foot into it now.

"The League is, well, the League. They only give information as is necessary for the safety of the public, and almost 100% of the time, they only give half of the full story."

Less than, if she's being honest.

"Is that why you're doing your dissertation on the rumors surrounding what happened?"

"Yes... and no. I don't know. I guess I just want to know what really happened."

"Lily, she was driven mad by magic fever. And the things people do during a mental breakdown? Well, it isn't them. Not really. The tribunal wrote a whole article on the dangers of magic sickness after it happened, and they rerun the article every year."

"You're probably right. I shouldn't think into it so much."

He turns her around, pulls her in until her breasts press flush against his chest. She's forgotten her gloves again. He breathes a long "haaaa" over her icy knuckles, warming them between his hands.

"Hey. I'm sorry about all this. I should've just told you. I may not have realized exactly where Kyle was taking us, but I knew it had something to do with hexen ghosts—but the Songstress herself!"

"It's fine, babe. Your intentions were good."

"You know what they say about the road to hell."

She chuckles. "I guess."

The glow of the fairy lights twinkle—starlight she can touch.

"This is what I was hoping we would see, though. It's rare enough to find fairies in the countryside. Good luck finding them in the city. You have to travel into the untouched parts of the world to see them."

"You mean into the dead zones where technology can't connect."

"Yes, into the dead zones where my girlfriend can't disappear into the network."

"It's not like I go anywhere when I'm connected, Sebastian."

"Maybe not physically, but you're like my students when we're reading a particularly riveting story. They disappear from the real world entirely, but that's the magic of story-telling. You can take anyone anywhere without ever leaving your home, and for the most part, it's totally legal. But with you, when you go into the network, you become someone else entirely. It's like you're more there than here. More outside yourself. I could watch you conduct your research for hours, you're so alive when in your element, but at the same time, I miss you terribly whenever you're in that other space."

Lily's chocolate–brown eyes avert down.

"I know it can be off–putting at times. I'm sorry—"

He takes her hand. "No, no, no. That's not what I'm saying, Lil. I love that you're augmented. I love that you're connected to this giant universe that I can't even comprehend. I love that you love being connected. I love how smart and fun and passionate you are. But most of all, I love you."

One of the more courageous fae titters forward. The little sprite dances around their heads, leaving sparkling halos of dust in its wake. It taps Lily on the shoulder before flitting away into the night. When she turns back to Sebastian, he's disappeared from her line of sight and dropped down onto one knee.

"Lily..."

Her breath catches in her heart.

"The last two years of my life have been the best I have ever lived. Meeting you, getting to know you, loving you has been the highlight of my life, and if you could humor this mere mortal of a man long enough to feel the same, then all I can do is ask..."

Sebastian pulls a small box from his coat pocket and opens it to reveal a simple silver band; inlaid at its center is a shimmering solitaire diamond.

"Lily Marie Esquire, will you marry me?"

Her heart hiccups as though struck by Cupid's arrow. Her tech systems register her as in distress, and she can see the light of the node on her wrist flickering like a flame in the wind.

"Yes, Sebastian. Yes, I'll marry you."

And she tackles him to the ground with a kiss.

The sound of a champagne cork popping echoes through the clearing, scattering the fairies dancing in the grass and sparking Lily away from her fiancé's lips. Kyle whoops as the fuzzy alcohol spills out onto the ground.

"Woohoo!! My lil bro is getting married!"

Beside him, Jeanine has her camera out; the flash goes off, catching Lily's smile.

"Congratulations!"

Javier and Derrick spin each other around as they race into the clearing to embrace both Sebastian and Lily in a hug.

"We won't be the only married fogies around here anymore. Let's see the ring. Is it as good as he said it would be?"

Lily turns to Sebastian in surprise. "You had all of this planned."

"Of course, I did. I wanted to make this special for you."

Kyle shakes the champagne bottle, aiming it up and spraying a rain of bubbly over all four of them.

"Now that we got that bit of business over with, let's fucking party! Happy Hexennacht, bitches!"

VIII

The Fog Descends

BOOZE FLOWS LIKE WATER AROUND THE campsite. Javier plays music from his phone through a pair of bluetooth speakers. Sebastian and Derrick have gathered stray branches and leaves to make a decent fire. Javier even unearths a set of masks he brought with him. It feels like a true Halloween celebration, complete with frivolity, merriment, and even a "haunted" witch's hut to sleep next to—not that Lily appreciates them sleeping anywhere near it.

After Lily ran off, the others set up camp by the dilapidated cottage. It's a small comfort to know they've all taken her warning seriously, and none of them are planning to sleep in the small house; Lily accepts the small olive branch.

Kyle wears the mask of a jester and twirls a fox mask–wearing Jeanine around the fire while Sebastian sways Lily back and forth at the edge of the glow. The whiskey is warm in her belly, her thoughts fuzzy around the edges, Sebastian's hands cool on her heated skin and the ring on her finger even cooler.

The fairies have long since flitted away.

As they dance, she trails her fingers along the rigid bark of the trees.

"You've just made me the happiest man in the world, Lily."

"Don't get too jolly," she teases, winking at him with a sloshy smile. "I'm still mad at you about this whole thing."

"Guess I should have stuck with the usual ring-in-the-champagne-glass-at-a-restaurant shtick." He tugs her closer to the fire, guiding her to sit on one of the picnic blankets.

"I wouldn't say you had to go that mundane, but some place with running water would have been nice."

"I promise I'll make it up to you."

She kisses him as he starts a one-handed massage on her neck. "I can't wait."

"I bet you can't. I'll have to pamper my fiancé."

And he plants a butterfly kiss at the nape of her neck.

"Anyone want to come swimming with me?" Jeanine calls.

The redhead shakes her head in answer while Javier squeaks in outrage

"Are you crazy! The water is gonna be freezing by now."

"Well, I'm going."

"Alright."

"I'll come with you," offers Kyle, following behind the girl. "Make sure nothing tries to drown her."

The jibe earns him a good-natured smack to the shoulder. Oh, Lord, she better not be fixing to have Jeanine as a sister-in-law.

But she'll worry about that later.

Sebastian's fingers work magic into the tense muscles of her shoulders, and her eyelids, weighted down by the day and the drink, fall shut.

"Lily..."

Whispers in the night, the sound of a fiddle playing over the water, and fairies dancing in the grass. She floats in an autumn breeze, light as a feather, unwilling to move, her bones stiff as a board on a pillow of mist.

"Lily..."

She drifts down the river toward the trill of the violin. Her own face stares back at her from the ripples of the water.

"Beware the river spirits, love. I hear they love to make a splash at parties."

A misty hand breaks the surface and reaches toward her face.

A scream frightens Lily awake. She doesn't even remember falling asleep. Around the campsite, the boys are all passed out as well. Kyle hugs a beer bottle, Javier hugs Derrick, and Sebastian is wrapped around her. But where is Jeanine? She went swimming, didn't she? But Kyle is back, so shouldn't she be back as well?

"Jeanine?"

Lily untangles herself from her fiancé, loudly hushing for the other girl.

"Over here."

The quietest of whispers responds, a voice that sounds like Jeanine but also doesn't.

"You alright?" she asks, moving toward the voice.

No answer comes.

There's a rustling sound in the bushes. The other girl's pack is still on the ground next to her tent. The pink backpack sits upright, untouched and unobtrusive. Jeanine's roll of toilet paper sits undisturbed atop her backpack.

Did she maybe go to the bathroom and forget her roll?

"Jeanine, you forgot the toilet paper."

She calls again to no answer, making her way to the edge of the camp with the roll of paper in hand.

It's much darker around the clearing than it should be with the fire still lit, the shadows seeming to stretch in the opposite direction of where they should.

As she steps past the radius of the campfire, her boot squishes into a wet spot on the ground. What the—? It hasn't rained, why is there water on the ground? Maybe from when they went swimming?

"Jeanine?"

"Psst!"

"Just stay there. I'm coming. "

Except when she reaches the tree line, a dark green crusted thing lunges at her chest. On trained instinct, she backhands the creature away with the metal inlaid part of her arm. It gives a human–like groan and disappears toward the lake, and she lands in a patch of damp earth.

"Jeanine, I swear if you—"

She wipes her hands on her jeans but instead of a dark brown smear of soil, she finds instead a ruddy red streak. Red has seeped into the ground all around her. A dark, viscous red disturbingly akin to the texture of blood.

"Jeanine!" she shouts, jumping to her feet. What the hell just attacked her?

"Lily? What's wrong?" Sebastian bolts awake at Lily's yell.

"There was this thing, Jeanine is missing, and I found blood."

"You found what?"

"Blood, Sebastian!"

Kyle, Javier, and Derrick jolt up.

"What's happening?"

"Fuck, when did we fall asleep?"

"Where's my sister?"

Upon finding his sister missing, Javier begins to hyperventilate.

"Weren't you with her?" asks Derrick, looking at Kyle.

"Well, yeah, but I don't remember coming back here."

"Lily, where is she?"

"I don't know. I woke up and she was gone and—"

"You woke up. How long have you been awake? Fuck, how long have we been asleep?"

"The last I checked it was 7 o'clock," says Derrick, checking his watch. "That's weird."

"What? What is, honey?"

"My watch is broken."

Derrick holds his arms up, and sure enough the analog watch on his wrist is completely busted. The glass of the face cracked, and the hour hand limply spins around its anchor point.

"How did that happen?"

"Does anybody else have a watch?"

Kyle tugs his multitool from his belt and, glancing at it, frowns.

"Alright. Whoever is playing a joke needs to cut their shit."

"Whoa, Kyle chill. No one's pranking anyone."

"Then explain to me why my clock is fucked up, too."

"Lily, do you have the time?" asks Sebastian.

Lily pulls up her interface. Lines of code appear before her visuals, flashing to remind her she's out of network range, but she should still be able to check what time it is. Only when she swipes open her date/time screen, the numbers are all scrambled.

"I can't get a time read, either."

"Fuck!"

Kyle's curse sends a flock of birds flying into the sky.

A distant scream.

"Jeanine!"

Lily takes off, sprinting toward the sound.

"Lily, wait!"

She runs scans on her systems as she goes. Hawthorne branches, peppercorn bush, poison oak, northern sugar maple, pine...so much pine. Pine needles, pinecones, pine thorns, scraping across her face and arms as she blindly barrels through them. Her system beeps at her in alarm, and she stops mere inches from tumbling over the edge of an overcrop. Below her, about ten feet down, black water churns. The lake.

"Jeanine, where are you?!"

No answer comes.

"Lily!"

Behind her, she hears the men shouting for her. Crap, in her haste to get to Jeanine, she completely left them behind. Now she's alone. No Jeanine. No Sebastian. Nobody.

"Over here!"

"Don't move. We're coming your way."

"Okay!"

She can hear them coming through the brush. It shouldn't take them too long to reach her. There are two trees to her left woven around each other, a lover's embrace in a whispering forest. If she tilts her head, it almost looks like the trees have faces, their branches arms reaching to curl around one another. Helpless fancies.

Just beyond the peculiar pair, something pale flits past, milky white and quick as a fleeing rabbit.

"Jeanine, is that you?"

A giggle greets her in response. A sweet, tinkling sound like daisies dancing in the wind.

"Jeanine, this isn't funny!"

The giggling fades into a cadenced hum, notes that rise and fall with the sound of the rustling leaves. The sounds of the forest rest almost in deference to the melody. The wind stills, the insects quiet, and Lily holds her breath.

Hmm hm hmmm hm hm... Hmm hm hmmm hmm hm hm hm.

Haunting and beautiful and climbing up the octave in a steady ascension of full steps intertwined with dissonant halves.

A song hummed by an invisible songstress.

Beneath her feet, the ground seems to pulse, mist curling around her feet and rising to thicken around her.

WARNING: MAGIC DETECTED

The fog shimmers with it. Wild, untamed magic, similar to the glittering dust of the fairies, but this is different. More somehow. Thicker, penetrating, the harsh unyielding nature of rock and stone and wood compared to the ever-shifting wash of water.

Blades of grass prick at her ankles, and when she looks, the previously wilted brush thickens and lengthens, rising taller with plant growth.

"Who's there?"

Her feet crunch alarmingly as she steps forward. Unthinking as though compelled she makes her way toward the music, toward the enchantment, using the trees to guide her footsteps. The fog folds around her, dense but thin, light yet heavy, suffocating yet the only thing filling her lungs.

Çlevær *uŋt mina...*

A whisper on the wind.

Çlevær *uŋt mina...*

A harp on the water.

Çlevær *uŋt mina...Come to me...*

A woman in the mist.

Golden locks, braided in flowers and crowned in brambles, fall around her shoulders to cascade over the swell of her naked breasts. Her milky white skin gleams in the moons' light. The soft swell of her stomach, the full curve of her hips, the smooth meld of her buttocks in her thighs. Venus! A living goddess in the middle of the woods singing an unearthly melody in a language Lily has never heard before, and she cannot look away.

The woman lifts her head. Eyes black as coal penetrate into her being. Reflected in those eyes is the quiet peace of a clock frozen in time.

"Lily, there you are."

And in the blink of an eye, the woman disappears.

"Sebastian."

Sebastian climbs his way over a fallen tree, Kyle close behind, Javier and Derrick pulling up the rear. Javier holds his side as he folds over, hands on his knees as he pants for breath.

"Can we not do that again?"

Lily looks back for the singing woman. She's gone. Vanished as easily as a dream.

"Are you alright?" asks Sebastian, his hand warm on her elbow.

Light burns her pupils as Kyle shines his flashlight into her face.

"I'm fine. We need to find Jeanine."

"It's pitch black out here. She can be anywhere. The farther we get from the camp, the more we risk getting lost ourselves. Better to wait until dawn and look for her when it's light out."

Javier coughs, trying and failing to speak before spitting on the ground, catching his voice as Derrick rubs his back.

"We can't just leave my sister in the forest alone."

"Baby, she probably just lost her way coming back from the loo. She's a smart girl; she'll know to stay put until morning when we can find her more easily."

"You call that scream getting lost?"

Derrick shrugs, looking at Javier. The man, hyperventilating, looks like he is about to have a panic attack. "I shouldn't have invited her to come."

"Jeanine is fine, babe."

"There was blood in the grass."

"Maybe she's on her period," scoffs Kyle.

"I'll give you a period," growls Lily, balling up a fist and thrusting it under Kyle's nose. What an asshole!

"You were the last person with her!"

Derrick steps in between with much the same idea as Lily. Sebastian tries to cut them both off. Kyle directs his aggression toward Derrick, and in the scuffle, Lily gets shoved sideways into a tree. Kyle punches Derrick in the stomach who in turn uppercuts him on the chin. Kyle spits blood out of his mouth and elbows Derrick in the face.

"You wanna go, you fucking organic? Watch me rip your fucking head off!"

"Kyle! Derrick!"

Sebastian pulls Kyle around to try and break the two up while Javier tries to grab Derrick.

"Guys, stop it! I don't think—Ah!"

Yanked off his feet with a sickening crack, Javier lands on his back, glasses flying from his face as he disappears into the underbrush with a scream.

"Javi!"

Derrick chases after his husband, dragged along the ground by some incorporeal force.

"Derrick, wait!"

Sebastian, Lily, and Kyle give chase, following Derrick's shouts. Derrick's cry of Javier's name cuts off with a sound like an axe hitting a tree.

IX

Spooky Scary Skeletons

THEY FIND KYLE'S AXE, BROKEN IN TWO and lying in a patch of bloodied leaves and blood-stained grass ripped from the ground. Derrick and Javier are nowhere in sight, and when Lily calls their names, her own voice, echoing back through the trees, is all the answer she gets.

Sebastian rounds on his brother. "You said you'd been here before. You said it was safe."

"It is safe. It's just a forest."

"Then what the hell took Derrick, Javi, and Jeanine?"

"I don't know."

"You don't know! You said you'd spent the night here. You said you scouted the place for danger."

"I lied, okay? I lied! I haven't fucking been here. Who in their right mind would come into Lorelei Forest alone? Do I look suicidal to you?"

Who in their right mind would come into Lorelei Forest at all?!

Kyle laughs in his brother's face. Fury boils in Lily's belly. Augmentations alight, and Lily rounds on the man, uncaring of the fact that he's Sebastian's older brother.

"You brought us here blind." Her fist meets his chest, the node on the back of her hand burning an aggravated red. "And you didn't even have the decency to be honest about it. You think you can use us as your fucking guinea pigs!"

"Get the hell off of me before I test just how good your goddamn augmentations are."

Spit flies into Lily's face, and she balls her hand in his shirt, ready to spit in his eye.

"Hey, hey! That's enough, you two. Fighting each other isn't going to help anything." Sebastian steps in between the two augmented humans, completely uncaring for his safety. He pulls Lily off his brother by the hip and shoves Kyle backward, keeping a hold of him by his coat collar. "Now, we are going to figure out what the hell we're going to do. Jeanine, Javi, and Derrick are missing, and we don't have the equipment we need to find them. Lily, are you able to send a message?"

Lily huffs, righting her clothing from the manhandling. "No. I'm completely cut off from any network."

"What good is having a computer in your head if you can't use it?" Kyle complains.

"I don't know. What good is having a cell phone if you're going to secretly lure a group of people into the middle of a forest that is known as one of the most haunted places on earth and therefore out of network range?"

Cowed, Kyle backs off.

"So, we make our way back to the cars, and from there, we can get to the network. Call for help, so we can find Jeanine, Javier, and Derrick."

It's the most sensible thing to do, rather than run around in the dark, so with the plan set, they pack up the bare minimum of items to go. At least, it sounds like a good plan. The execution of it leaves much to be desired. When KC refuses to turn on at Kyle's command, they are forced to take even less gear in hand to head for the exit.

They get nowhere. Literally nowhere. The forest seems to shift and change around them, a labyrinthine biosphere, and they are at the center of it. Kyle has his compass out and insists they are heading the right direction, but her scanners read the same landmarks over and over again.

"Kyle, do you even know where you are going?"

"I'm telling you. It's this way."

"This is the third time I've seen that fallen tree in an hour."

"It can't be the same tree. We haven't made any turns, and the moons have been on our right this whole time."

"It's the same tree."

"Baby, Kyle's right. We haven't made any turns. I've been keeping an eye on the compass."

Falling quiet, Lily scowls and follows since that is apparently what is expected of her. She tracks the sky, watching the moons dance across the dome, or rather, watching the moons *not* dance across the dome. The minutes tick by and Koi and Dei remain ever stagnant in the sky. Suddenly she is made aware of just how quiet the forest has become.

"Guys?"

"Now what?" gruffs Kyle. Sebastian gives him a "dude, chill" look.

"What is it, Lily?"

"Something is wrong."

"How horror–movie cliche of you…"

Kyle scoffs, already shaking his head as he keeps marching the same direction.

"I'm serious."

"I'm sure you are, sweetheart, but I know where I am. I told you. Why can't you just trust me?"

"Because this is the fourth time we've passed the same fallen tree, and you're not listening to me."

"It isn't the same fucking tree!"

"No, Kyle. I think it is."

Sebastian stares down at the fallen wood as though he was looking at a death sentence. He kneels down and pulls directly from the bark...one of his rainbow nose strips.

"I left this the last time we passed it."

"That's not possible."

"Kyle, I'm telling you, that's what I did."

"No! That's not possible!"

In a mad outburst, Kyle takes off running. Lily tries to chase after him, but Sebastian stops her as mere seconds later, Kyle runs back into them from the opposite direction he left. Hazel eyes wide with shock, the man heaves a breath, hands coming up to clench at his hair.

"What the fuck..."

"Kyle, calm down, man. We need to figure out what is going on—"

"What the fuck!!" He swings, narrowly missing Sebastian's face, to nail a tree dead center. "I'm going to tear apart these goddamn woods!"

"Kyle, don't!"

Kyle's mechanical fist meets the tree trunk, leaving a dent in the wood and punctuating his words as he strikes over and over and over again.

"I'm so..."

Punch!

"...sick of this..."

Punch!

"...goddamn forest!"

Punch!

He slams his fist into the wood over and over and over again until the tree topples sideways, collapsing into its neighbor with a shattering of wood and leaves.

"Kyle, stop it!"

The sound that spills from the man's mouth is bestial and primitive as he zeros in on the next tree, rearing a fist back with enough power to send a hole through the thick trunk. But before the hit can land, a branch swings out. Thwack!

The branch catches him across the chest and tosses him backward as though he weighs no more than a miniature poodle.

"What the—"

The branches continue to swing wildly, Lily and Sebastian backing up even farther until the wood creaks back into place minus a few pockets of leaves.

"The forest is defending itself."

"But how can it—"

An inhuman trill echoes through the night, a cross between an owl's screech and a wolf's howl.

"What was that?"

Lily's scans sift through the analytic systems in her head looking for an explanation for the sound neither animal nor hexen.

"I don't know, but it isn't human."

"Whatever it is, I'm going to rip it in two."

Exhaust ports along the man's mechanical arms ripple with orange light. The machinery whirs and hisses as he charges up, ready to go after the next thing that moves.

"Kyle, calm down," says Lily. "We have no idea what it is."

"You stay out of this."

"I said leave her alone, Kyle!"

Sebastian comes up behind his brother and grabs him by his mechanical arm.

"Sebastian!"

Kyle swings back, slamming Sebastian across the chest. There's a sick crunching sound as Sebastian's back hits a tree. Lily runs to Sebastian; he's unconscious.

"Oh, fuck! Bassy?"

His head lolls to the side in her hands, unresponsive.

"Bassy! I didn't mean to—Shit! Lily, is he going to be okay?"

"Shut up, Kyle!" Lily looks for Sebastian's pulse. His breathing is shallow, his heart rate disturbingly slow. "Sebastian. Sebastian, look at me. Open your eyes, baby."

Sebastian's lashes tremble as his eyes open, a weak flutter like the wings of a dying butterfly.

"Lily…"

Oh, thank god!

"Lily, it—it hurts."

"I know. I know it does, baby. I'm going to get you help. It's going to be okay."

But she can't make that promise herself. They have no more first aid supplies, no way of contacting help, so she composes an S.O.S. in her head and sends it.

MESSAGE DELIVERY FAILED

Try again.

DELIVERY FAILED

Again!

NETWORK CONNECTION UNAVAILABLE

Damn it! Keep trying!

A twig snaps to her right. Kyle's flashlight swings around to focus on the sound.

"Who's there? Who the fuck is there? Come out!"

"Kyle, stop it!"

A branch creaks to her left, and she jumps to her feet, one foot on either side of Sebastian's body. That was too close. Disconcertingly close. Lily's scanners are going crazy, identifying trees and roots and insects in microseconds but unable to pinpoint the source of the sound or catch the glimpse of a pale body darting through the darkness.

"I said come out, so I can rip your fucking head off!"

Hwroohwroo… Hwroohwroo…

The hooting call of an owl is the only reply he receives, and the quiet settles like a thick fog over the area. So still Lily holds her breath.

"I swear to God whoever the fuck is doing this I'll—Argh!"

Something jumps onto Kyle's back. Something humanoid and angry. Matted locks of hair whip from side to side as Kyle thrashes. Kyle's flashlight sails through the air, hitting a tree and dying.

"Kyle!"

Snarls and hisses punctuated by the man's screams.

"Get it off me!"

The creature's back is bark–like and rough, and Lily's fingernails scrape painfully against it as she tries to pull the creature off. A metal prong opens on her wrist, and she strikes the attacker across the back of the head, dislodging it and sending it racing into the woods before she can get a good look at it.

"What the hell was that! A ghost?!"

No. It couldn't have been a ghost. She'd touched it. Some sort of fae or hexen? She turns back to Sebastian only to find him gone.

"Sebastian?"

Lily scrambles to turn on the torch implant at her wrist. The LED bulb, no bigger than her pinkie nail, flickers on, washing the area in white light. The grass angrily rustles where he once laid, the indentation of his body still carved through the ground.

The leaves of a bush fold back into place. A furry tawny–colored tail disappears with a hiss.

"Sebastian!" Lily runs into the night after Sebastian, the beam of her flashlight burning from tree to tree. Why didn't she ever get night vision implants?

"Lily, wait!"

"Sebastian!"

A pitched shriek answers her.

"Don't you hurt him!"

The forest shifts around her despite the rigidness of the night, oppressive and penetrating to her. Creaking in the trees and screams in the night as the woods close in around her. A sharp branch cuts across her cheek. Her breath steams in the frigid air, turning to icicles before her eyes. It shouldn't be this cold. Not even this far north. Not when the solstice is still two months off.

Crack!

"Ahh!"

Pain alights in her ankle, and Lily tumbles heels over head into the dirt. She lands with a squelching sound, her hands sinking into the mud and leaf litter. The roots spring up. Jagged wood winds around her torso, tugging her deeper into the frozen ground. The damp of decay seeps into her socks, and fire flairs across her wrist as a red–tailed centipede crawls over her skin.

She yanks herself out of their grip, pulling up grass and decaying leaves.

"Lily, stop! You don't know where you're going."

Kyle chases after her.

"I have to save Sebastian!"

She keeps running, the air pumping into her lungs with the aid of her O2 supplementary augmentation until the bulk of a half–mechanical body tackles her from behind. She falls with a shout, and she and Kyle go tumbling down an incline.

"Listen to me, you little tramp. My brother wanted to bring you out here to propose, and now he's missing."

A mechanical palm slaps her across the face.

"He's missing because of you, you prick! You hit him hard enough to break his ribs. You might have killed him, and now he's gone because you thought it would be a good idea to go for a stupid ghost tour!"

She knees him in the stomach. He curses, rolling off her as she gets her hands and feet under her. A boot flies into her side. She catches his ankle and tugs him off his feet. He falls to the ground, heavy as a boulder with a grunt. The bigger they are... Metal fingers clamp down on her head and tug her sideways.

"Your augmentations are trash, girlie."

He bears down, pressure building painfully in her head.

"Let go!"

"You're going to turn on that fucking computer in your head and get someone out here to help me find my baby brother. Do you understand me? I don't buy that bullshit you're on about the network. I've seen technomancers work from less."

"Argh! I'm not a technomancer!"

"You could've been!"

"That doesn't mean—"

A high–pitched squeal zips past her elbow into Kyle's eyes. Dust and glitter fly into Kyle's eyes. He lets her go with a roar of pain. Hwrooooo!

The blur of a Great Grey Owl flashes across Kyle's head, talons flashing red in the moonlight.

"My eye!"

He collapses, clenching his face. Lily scrambles backward as growls rip through the trees. A meaty flank knocks her sideways, and the back of her skull meets a rock. Two wolves rush forward, lunging for Kyle. One of them, sharp teeth glinting white, bites down on the soft tender flesh of his throat. He gurgles as the other rips into his side.

She blinks, and Kyle's bloodied outline blurs. The two wolves become three and a half, and into her line of sight, a pale human figure steps forward. Tall, angular, walking on their toes like a gargoyle or feline. A tail flicks agitated behind them.

A blink of her eye, and the woman is before her, inhuman eyes glaring at her. Before Lily can react, the creature's hands close on her forearm, human but not human hands, nails dirtied and gnarled from the wilderness. She yanks her arm up and sharp teeth bite down, burying deep into the meat of her forearm. Fire ignites along the limb, boiling hot like acid spilled from a testing beaker.

And the stars blink out.

Lily's eyes open, heavy and crusted as though she has been sleeping for hours. The moons hang high in the sky, Dei—full as usual while Koi hangs in an upturned crescent—a Cheshire Cat grin. *We're All Mad Here.*

But where is "here"?

Kiss, Kiss, Kiss

Nine Years Ago – 12th Day in the Month of Storms, 1861 A.P. – The 247th Technomancer Trials – Shinka Temple

"I AM ASSIGNING YOU A PARTNERED TASK. You shall work in pairs on your final project. Either you both pass with full colors, or you both fail. There is no one or the other. I fully expect you to assimilate yourselves with a participant from a different background and/or nation than you."

Finnick Lockcrafte is a burly old goat. Probably the most famous technomancer of his age for his prowess in slaying vampyres and werewolves, he is also the most antisocial person Lily has ever met, so receiving a group project from this man is, to put it mildly, unexpected.

To their credit, none of the participants groan. There are only a few murmured whispers of disdain, namely from the Derivan and Sekhmetian students. So close to the end of the theoretical portion of the Summit, they are, and everyone is ready for the final project, though none of them expected a partnered assignment to be the crux of their theoretical assessments.

The moment Lockcrafte says to disperse, she turns around to face Rhiannon and Lydia while Selene and Wren wander over from their seats closer to the Ebelean and Derivan participants respectively. And that's when Lily realizes they have a problem. From their group of friends, Heather has already been dismissed, and Wren, making her way over from beside her brother, seems to realize the situation as well.

There's an awkward moment when the five of them all look sheepishly between themselves because unfortunately 5 doesn't divide evenly by 2.

"Maybe one of you could work with my brother. I'm sure Xipilli wouldn't mind if—" Wren cuts herself off midsentence as her brother fist bumps Chike. "Nevermind. The bromance continues between Xipilli and my future brother–in–law."

"What if we asked Irene?"

Except when Lily turns to find the girl, she's already partnered up with a girl from Ebele.

"Oh, look Lionheart's coming over."

The next few minutes that unfold are the most painstaking moments Lily has ever experienced. Her face warms, a blush rising into her cheeks as she averts her eyes.

"My lady, I'm sure we could finish this project with an all–nighter or two."

"Well, I..."

"What do you say, *mon cherie*?"

Only when she looks up, Lionheart isn't talking to her. He's talking to Wren.

Lily has never known what it feels like to be stabbed in the heart, and she might be being overdramatic, but this might be the closest she's ever come to that. But Wren isn't even looking at Lionheart. Despite his attempt to woo her with the usage of a Derivan endearment, she's staring past him.

One of the other girls has approached Kaito, seemingly to be his partner. He doesn't rebuke her, but he doesn't exactly seem accepting of her either. She sits down anyway, leaning into his space and setting her hand on his shoulder. Her hands squeeze the teen's shoulder in mimicry of a massage. At this point, the prince says something about pursuing a particularly complex theorem for the final presentation. It seems to deter her because she quickly retreats from the man's side, veering back to a group of giggling girls, leaving the Miyazaki teen alone once again.

"You think they'll make an exception for someone if no one wants to work with them?" Lydia whispers to Lily.

"Don't you mean if they don't want to work with anyone else?" inserts Selene with a laugh.

Wren rises from her seat.

"Sorry, Lionheart. I don't think you and I have the same definition of an all-nighter."

The boy stutters. "Well, hold on. I—"

Lionheart's jaw drops, stunned, as Wren angles around him, wishing the other girls good luck on their projects, and makes her way to the vacated seat next to Kaito.

"What is she doing? I thought he couldn't stand her."

"Maybe she wants to test the limits of her mortality for her final project."

Only instead of being rebuked like the last girl who approached Kaito, she settles into the seat across from him, activates her mechanical hand's holoscreen, and begins plotting something or other for the assignment. For his part, the prince doesn't say anything, simply turns his head toward her, activates his sights, and reaches out to make an adjustment on her holo.

"Xipilli is going to throw a fit," says Selene, stunned.

"Xipilli," starts Rhiannon, "is going to have a piece of my mind if he bothers his sister for her choice in partner."

Lionheart stands speechless for a long second. He must not be very practiced at handling rejection.

"So, uh, Lily. Would you like to be my partner?"

Lily starts at the boy's address. He gives her a winning smile—the same smile that convinced her to spend the night with him just a few days ago. She won't be fooled by it this time.

"Sorry, but Lydia and I are already working together."

The Murasaki girl, at the mention of her name, giggles.

"Oh yeah, sorry, Lionheart. This one's spoken for."

Lydia flings an arm around Lily's shoulders, and Lily learns something that day that she won't soon forget.

Boys suck.

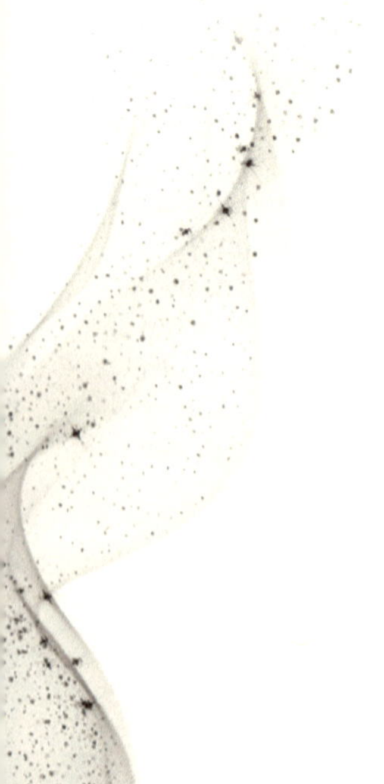

XI

Dead on Arrival

THE FOREST IS GONE, REPLACED INSTEAD by four walls, furniture, and the thin, naked trunk of a willow that stretches upward through the roof only to weep down around her. Lily lies on her back in a bed, a dusty, old double draped in gauzy netting, torn and yellowing with age. Blinking up at the half–broken circular canopy, where she expects to see ceiling and timber, there is instead a hole torn out by the tree growing through the center of the room. Starlight and moonbeams trickle through the incomplete blackness. Hanging from the canopy ring are several crystals, hung from ribbon and string as well as a child's necklace and a torn–up picture colored in crayons and markers.

Her fingers go numb as she realizes where "here" is. The cottage. In the back bedroom. In a bed not her own. A bed that once belonged to a witch. A very dead witch. She's been sleeping in the bed of a dead witch.

Jolting up with a shriek, she scrambles for the door, tripping over the hem of a long nightgown. What the hell? This isn't hers. It's threadbare and motheaten, like it hasn't been worn in years. Oh God! It hasn't been worn in years. Surely, this isn't *hers*! She woke up in Wren's bed wearing Wren's clothes. She gets up, the hem tearing, but just as she reaches the door, the wood slams shut, vines winding around the paneling, locking it in place. She pushes and pulls at the handle, but it isn't until she slams her shoulder into the rotting wood that she falls plain through it. Crawling to the front door, vines lash at her calves, thorns scratching into the meat of her shin. One of the spines pierce the center of one of the nodes on her leg. Electricity shocks through the plant, warding it away as she pulls herself backward by her elbows.

The vines wither and die at her feet, but the anguished cry of pain comes from behind her.

Out of the mist, a woman steps, naked but for the foliage woven around her torso. Like a creature from a fairy tale, she drifts over the mossy earth as intangible as the mist from whence she unfolded. Her hair is matted and tangled through with leaves, her skin milky pale, eyes like obsidian gems in her narrow face. Behind her flicks a long bovine tail of the purest white, and over her back ripples the roughened patterns of tree bark. In an instant of clarity, Lily realizes this creature is not merely of the forest. She is the forest. The woman's lips part, and she ducks her head between her knees as the sound that spills forth cripples her.

The ear–splitting falsetto of a huldra's scream.

A thorn pierces through her mind, wedging its way into the very center of Lily's skull. Mites dance up her arms, the bugs crawl under her skin, eat at her sinew, and from their fatted corpses, seedlings sprout. Seedlings which take root in her bones and marrow. The roots replace her skeleton and brambles her hair. Her skin becomes as rough and hard as tree bark and her voice becomes the rustling leaves.

The screaming stops.

Lily gasps, once again herself. Ripped from the hallucination, she feels her face and throat. No tree bark. Her hair is soft and golden. Her body is flesh and blood and bone. Not plant matter. Not compost.

Lily's tech system is going on the fritz. Her internal servers whine at her to retreat, vacate, run away. But there is nowhere to run. This huldra will hunt her down and kill her. Kill all of them. Damnit, why did Kyle have to bring an axe into the woods?

The huldra watches her. The woman looks at Lily, crouched where she is on the ground, curled up with her hands over her ears. Carefully, Lily lifts her head and meets the woman, this queen of the forest, eye to eye.

"I'm sorry we came into your forest. I'm sorry we hurt your trees."

She looks at Lily with those eyes, like shark's eyes, cold and calculating. Her head cocks to one side like an owl or a hawk. Can she understand Lily? Does she even speak common? Does it matter? Her tech nodes flash in the dark, normally a cool pink, now red with distress.

The huldra trills a chirrup sound the whole forest vibrates to.

"Please, let my friends go, and I promise you we will never trespass on your forest again. It was a mistake for us to come here."

MESSAGE SENT

Something got through. Her S.O.S. went through. To whom? Which network did she connect to? Who cares! Hurry, whoever is seeing this message. Please, hurry!

The huldra hisses, stepping toward her.

She's going to kill her. She's going to kill all of them.

With her eyes screwed shut, she counts the creature's footsteps on the grass. 1...2... light as a bunny and equally quiet. 3...4...5... Leaves crunch right beside her, and she bows her head down.

"Please, I'm so, so sorry."

The huldra leans down. Fingertips thread through her hair, cold and smelling of damp earth. They catch in the tangles behind her ear and slowly unravel the knots, almost careful, as though she is trying not to hurt her.

"I'll do whatever you want. Just please let us go."

The huldra's head tilts, her left ear coming to her left shoulder. Her fingers smell like dirt and leaf litter and drip with enough power to pull Lily's skull from her spine.

She closes her eyes and prays.

BrrBeep!

KC barrels her way across the clearing like a deus ex machina (No, a machina ex deus!) ramming into the fae's legs, throwing her off balance, and Lily races away from the creature into the forest. A blind dash through the woods interrupted only by the shiny chrome painting of KC's metal shell.

"KC, activate reconnaissance systems."

A responding series of chirps greet her. The drone is on high alert searching for her missing friends, and Lily runs, following behind KC's taillight, blinking red in the darkness, not stopping until she nearly trips over the little bot as it comes to a sudden halt in front of a massive oak tree.

Its trunk is as thick as a dining room table, branches reaching up so high they disappear into the descending fog. The leaves shimmer golden in the dark, wild magic alive and pulsing through its branches, through the vines lacing up its trunk, and through its roots to bleed into the soil.

Still panting from her mad dash, Lily steps toward the tree. Her sensors go haywire as she sets a hand on the bark. This tree is old. Older than possibly even the bones of the first witches who migrated to Deus. Its unparalleled majesty is marred only by the charred, fire–blackened stain along its left side and the warding talismans hanging from the dead wood there. And at the base of this scar sit a handful of differently sized glass globes, all containing a single purple flower, the petals of which glow bioluminescent in the night light.

Another kind of magic, a blending of earth and sea. Like a saltwater lily.

"Nngh!"

A groan draws her attention, and her gaze darts up to find a network of vines and brambles crisscrossing over deathly pale skin. Her breath hitches, and she climbs toward that patch of flesh, anchoring herself on a branch as thick around as a tire. Clawing at the bark and pulling up moss and brambles, her nails catch on the thick ridges and crack down the middle, but she keeps digging, keeps ripping into the tree until her fingers tangle in long black hair.

"Jeanine?"

A sleepy moan greets her.

"Oh God, Jeanine! I'm here. It's Lily. I'm here. I'm going to get you out of there."

But the brambles grow back too quickly, snaking over Jeanine's chest and face before Lily can free her. Damnit! So, she draws her utility knife from her belt.

"I'm sorry."

The blade stabs into the tree trunk, and the forest shudders around her. The smell of rain and compost, earth and mud, damp wood and ozone sloshes past her as she hacks into the thick wood until finally Jeanine's body falls limply from the wooded cavern into her arms.

"Jeanine, open your eyes. Can you hear me?"

A weak whimper is all the answer she gets, drowned out by the whistling of the wind. Lily unhooks the flashlight from the bioelectric charging port on her hip and clicks it to life. The beam traces over the wood.

"Javier... Derrick... Kyle..."

They're all here. All of them, coiled into the tree by plant matter, all of them ghastly pale, looking like ghosts themselves against the dark of the ancient oak. Javier is curled into his husband's side as though they were caught together. Kyle bears no markings of the wolf attack earlier. In fact, even his clothes are different, matching what he wore before everything started to go ass up. And lastly, scruffy facial hair, curly blonde hair, and a chest decorated with a rainbow unicorn silhouette.

"...Sebastian."

Lily lays Jeanine down, cushioning her head with her jacket before getting up to cut Sebastian and the others from the tree. As she readies the blade, a pitched shriek rips through her synapse. Hands over her ears, she falls backward, landing on her back in the dirt.

He swims before her vision: Sebastian but not Sebastian. Sebastian, dead and rotting, surrounded by worms and roaches. Kyle, cold and still, mouth agape as a bat tugs out his tongue, mechanical arm broken and caked with rust. Jeanine, Javier, Derrick, pale, bloodless, fingers rigid with rigor mortis. Her own face, nose rotted away, eyes melted from her skull, a ghastly thing in a sylvan casket of thorns, a cadaver pillowed by autumn leaves.

"No!"

She crumples to her knees as thorns drill into her head. Or maybe they aren't thorns so much as they are worms—flesh-eaters feasting on her gooey white matter until all that's left is gelatinous slush. It feels like her skull is going to collapse on itself, sucked into a vacuum of her own dreams and desires until she is naught but baser, animalistic want.

"Stop it!!"

Crows take flight at her scream, and the silence that replaces their startled caws crackles with energy, like the aftershocks of an explosion or a bomb. The magic of the forest draws from her psyche, leaving her shivery and weak, her bones rattling like beads in a glass jar as she opens her eyes.

Kyle stands before her, blood dripping from his throat and arms, but it can't be Kyle. Kyle is buried in the trunk of the tree behind her.

The Kyle-shaped creature stoops down; its breath, putrid and smelling like rotting meat, ghosts over Lily's face. She gags on it, coughing up maggots as a clawed hand wraps around her throat.

"What are you?"

It's lips twist into a sharp–toothed grimace, revealing rows of pointed fangs sharp enough to rend her meat from her bones.

"What are you!"

The creature's maw opens to take a bite out of her when the huldra screams into its side, sending the other fae rolling off of Lily. That's when she realizes this huldra is protecting her. This is the huldra's tree. She was protecting them all! The two creatures scuffle, ripping into each other with teeth and nails and magic. The shapeshifter, bigger and wider than the huldra, gains the upper hand, knocking the woman onto her back. Lily scrambles up, a stone in hand to bash the shifter's head in, but a ghostly claw wraps around her throat, lifting her off her feet in a magical hold.

The huldra cries out. The creature's face, now more impish than human, twists with rage. Lily's vision darkens, her oxygenation system keeping her respiratory system going despite the crushing force on her windpipe, but it won't last for long.

SYSTEM SHUTDOWN IMMINENT – UNBLOCK AIRWAY TO AVOID

KC beeps erratically, throwing debris at the monster to no effect. She's going to die. She's going to die in this forest.

A blinding flash of violet floods her vision. The phantom hand disappears from her throat, a high–pitched shrill sounding from whatever the creature is. A shapeshifter of some kind? A hexen or a trickster fairy? She doesn't know. She doesn't care. All she cares about is the fact it now lies face down in the dirt with a katana buried in its back. A very familiar katana with state–of–the–art cabling connecting its hilt to its master.

Its master who stands draped in pale gray and lavender at the edge of the clearing.

XII

The Kiss of Dawn

"KAITO?"

Kaito Miyazaki turns to her, his robes rustling in the wind. His sights spin in his eyes, a vibrant violet in the darkness.

"Miss Esquire," he says, pulling Tsukuyomi from her now dead attacker. At the formal address of her name, Lily remembers herself, folding into a bow appropriate to bestow a man of his rank and station. The crown prince of Murasaki no Yama, a technomancer hailed as one of the most powerful in all of the League. "I received your S.O.S. You should not have come into this forest."

She's lucky he was even within range to receive her transmission. She must have picked up his private network and her League permissions granted her emergency transmission.

"*Hveðrungr* don't take kindly to intruders who enter their forests without permission. You're lucky the huldra interfered."

Hveðrungr—The roarer. Of course! A trickster fae known for its shapeshifting abilities, often mistaken for doppelgangers. It probably took on Kyle's shape early on, so when the wolves attacked Kyle, they were actually attacking the *hveðrungr*. The wolves must answer to the huldra, the unspoken queen of the forest. Speaking of the fae, the huldra is gone, disappeared into the forest, no doubt to avoid coming face to sword with the prince.

"I've uploaded a route to your drone's servers. It will lead you out of the forest."

"I'm not leaving them."

From the trees, several adepts dressed in Murasaki colors of wine and burgundy filter into the area. One of them approaches the Miyazaki prince and bows.

"Be mindful of the forest. Harm nothing."

"Yes, your highness."

The adept moves toward the great tree as Kaito addresses her once more.

"My adepts will see to it your friends are taken care of. You should pack your things and leave."

"I understand what you're saying, your highness, but if it's all the same to you, I'll wait."

"Hm," he hums in acknowledgement.

"How were you in range to receive my transmission?"

What are you doing here, your highness?

Kaito looks at her with colorless gray eyes as his adepts begin to coax her friends down from the trees. The adepts don't take long, carefully extracting them from the tree as gingerly as possible, making sure no harm comes to the ancient oak. They are so cautious, the wildlife, countless birds and beasts who vacated the area during the ruckus of her fight with the *hveðrungr*, returns. Owls call to each other in the trees, the crickets take up their autumn song, and even a few thumb–sized fairies flit into the space, dusting over the trans-humans as they work.

When they finally pull Sebastian from the bark, Lily hurries forward to check him over as they strap him into a gurney.

"Li–ly…"

He's awake, fingers lifting idly to touch her. *Oh, Sabastian!*

"Shh. Rest. They'll take care of you now." She looks to the adept as he closes his eyes. "He has broken ribs. Please be careful."

"It's alright, ma'am. We've given him a stim. He should be just fine in a few hours."

"Thank you."

The hveðrungr is rolled into a body bag, and when the last of the adepts prepares to vacate the area, she bows to Kaito, reporting something to him in Hanasu. The prince acknowledges her with a tilt of his head and a polite dismissal before she pivots and makes to leave. Lily makes to follow with KC but pauses. Kaito remains unmoving.

The man stands still as a statue, gazing up to the sky.

Her internal clock activates. 3AM. The witching hour is at hand, the time when gloomtide reigns and even the most devout of technomancers have gone to bed. All except one, that is.

Instead of following the path out of the forest, Kaito turns to the great tree, drifting over the grass like a pale wraith, such a contrast to the deep, rich colors his adepts wear. Why does he not wear the same colors as his underlings?

"Are you coming, your highness?"

He doesn't answer her, turning instead to regard the charred patch of earth and wood. A place where magic is so richly embedded in everything else, here is this one dead spot. Almost like walking into a deadzone, but worse. Instead of just her augmentations lacking the ability to connect, her very person feels like it is missing something. Like her very essence is being pulled out and syphoned into nothingness.

She wonders if Kaito feels it too.

The prince kneels, his lavender robes blacking with dust and dirt. From his pack, he pulls a glass orb. Half full of water and decorated with colorful coral paints, in the center of the orb floats a single amethyst sea lily in full, bioluminescent bloom, a matching addition to the others already settled around the gnarled tree.

An amethyst sea lily. Wren's favorite flower set at the base of this tree by Kaito Miyazaki, a man long known to have had a relationship with the witch. A relationship rumored to have continued even after she defected from the League— even though such gossip was quickly squashed by the technomancer council and the man's own brother as soundly as a hammer could flatten a nail.

"This is where she died, isn't it?"

A stupid question, really. Why else would he be here? Kneeling in the dirt. Him a prince, taking a weekend venture to arbitrarily bring flowers to a random tree, dress it as a grave, and make sure the spirits in the area are quelled enough to rest in peace. To make sure the spirit of his lost lover can rest in peace after dying in such a horrible manner.

"Is it true that Wren killed herself?"

The reports say as much, and they burned her body against a magical tree, probably in an effort to destroy its influence on the forest as well. They burned the witch but failed to fell the tree.

"I didn't know whether to believe it or not at first. Wren was always so sunny." Ever smiling, ever dreaming. She was the kind of person you knew would change the world, and she did. Lily just never expected she would change it like this. "You must have really lov—"

"Miss Esquire, if you please."

"Yes, my apologies. I'll leave you in peace."

With one last glance at the sigils painted across the shiny new talismans, Lily backs away from the man to follow KC silently buzzing in the direction of the exit. By the time she sets foot on the dirt road, gaining sight once more of her fiancé's truck and the emergency transports fixing to take her friends to the nearest hospital, the sun is just beginning to peek over the horizon, filtering through the autumn leaves in a kaleidoscope of warm, tangy oranges and yellows.

She looks back just once.

In the light of dawn, Lily Esquire bids thanks to the huldra who kept her friends alive, goodbye to Kaito Miyazaki, goodbye to Lorelei Forest, and goodnight to the Songstress of Lorelei.

May she find the peace in death she couldn't find in life.

The huldra sits in the shadows at the edge of the clearing, watching as the adepts carry out the fools who encroached on her forest. The five of them will live, her sacred tree having kept them alive. The girl was nearly drowned by the *nøkken*, and the tall burly one is lucky the trolls didn't grind his bones to dust. Hel, a *draugr*, almost sucked the life out of the skinny glasses wearing one. The wannabe cyborg with the mechanical arm is in the worst shape, no big grievance in her book—he hurt her trees—but a trip to a League hospital will fix him right up. The *hveðrungr* got him and took on his shape, but Jessabelle's wolves ate at least a piece of the misaligned fae. She can never begrudge them a meal, and the technomancer's blade did the rest.

Now the forest quiets once more as the invasive species shows itself out. All but one of them anyway.

"Really, Prince. Every year, you come here and offer incense to the place she died. What are you expecting will happen? That she'll appear and give you a kiss from the other side of the veil?"

The man, silent as the makeshift grave erected for his lost love, cannot hear her. She is too far away from him. Not that she expects him to understand her anyway. She doesn't speak common or Hanasu, so the words she spits at him are the most loving of Eldritch, the only spoken language she knows, learned during her time with Jessabelle, the language of magic and beasts of the nether planes. The fae speak it a little. Kara, the huldra who fell in love with a witch, only speaks it because of Jessabelle.

But she's willing to wager, even if he could understand her, he would remain just as mute. Ever the stoic Kaito Miyazaki. The brooding warrior, forever mourning his lost love. Some people might call him steadfast. Her, on the other hand... she could puke. He's such a walking cliche.

"I suppose you're too smart to expect such things but really. It's been five years. Shouldn't you have found yourself some pretty little wife by now? Shouldn't you at least give your time to someone with a pulse?"

The huldra's words, though scathing, are not said in unkindness. He's not the only one who has lost a witch, after all.

The incense he burns is foul-smelling and poignant, harsh on her nose hairs, and it makes her eyes water, but she doesn't shriek at it. Once a year, every year since the raid that nearly destroyed her land, he comes without fail. Why he chooses this day rather than the anniversary of her death or perhaps even the woman's birthday is beyond her. But she supposes Hexennacht is an appropriate time to visit the closest thing to a grave for a witch who was never given the honor of a funeral.

But she supposes if she were going to suffer the presence of any human or posthuman in this case, this one is a reasonable choice. He is quiet and unobtrusive. He doesn't kill the animals under her charge or spoil the soil with garbage. He's always mindful of the trees, and on occasions like today, when fools wander into her midst in need of rescuing, he ensures the grounds are left pristine in the wake of the people under his command.

The prince kneels holding vigil as the minutes pass on the witching hour. He doesn't speak or do anything outside of cleaning the grave and offering his brought flowers. Perhaps this is the reason she tolerates him: because the flowers complement her natural magic. The glowing blues, greens, and purples striking and cool against the golden shimmer of her tree. She knows they aren't really for her. They're for a dead witch, but she'll accept them anyway. It's not like the woman can claim the lilies for herself anyway.

Eventually though, he rises. He bows in her direction, saying something in a tongue she doesn't understand but understands implicitly.

"You think I watch over this place for your witch? Don't make me laugh!"

No, she does not guard this forest for any witch. She guards this forest from the humans not for the sanctity of any grave or cottage.

Humans are an invasive species. They plunder and pillage, and too many of them traipsing through her woods would kill the magic remaining in this place as surely as any nuclear bomb. An influx of people would have the animals scurrying off in fright at the mere sound of footsteps, birdsong would be drowned out by noise, and Gods forbid they set up any permanent settlement; the stink of sewage and waste would burn away the natural scent of earth and maple. A magic spell, beautiful and untouched, broken by too much humanity in one place. Not to mention the greater, darker truth...

Humans never arrive alone. With them, come Death and Destruction, following behind like pets on a loose leash.

Destruction dogs humanity's footsteps, ever hungry for the best strips of meat, ringing the bell and waiting to be hand-fed its breakfast, and after Destruction follows Death, a starved shadowy thing scavenging for scraps.

Both had followed the Songstress of Lorelei, a techno-mancer-turned-witch. She never fed them herself. Never put food in their mouths, was as caring and careful of the forest as Jessabelle had been, yet still they panted after her, starving and rabid by the end, and look what happens when starving hounds are let off their leash.

"It's her fault Jessabelle is dead."

Falsetto In The Woods

Even as she hisses the words, she knows they aren't true. Anger spitting lies. Wren was as responsible for Jessabelle's death as she is responsible for the sunrise, but...
Bitterness is sometimes a symptom of grief.

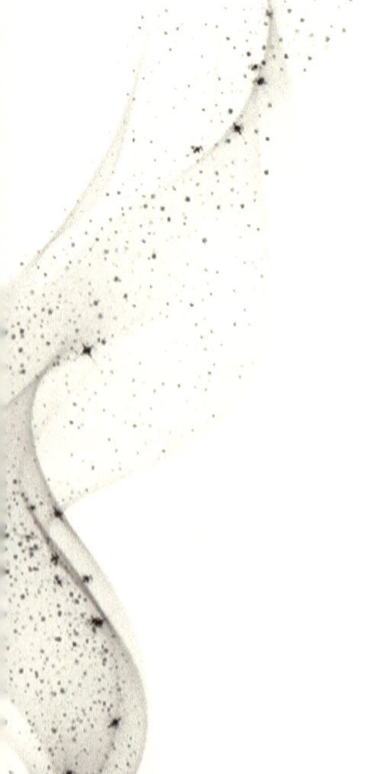

Index

The Thirteen Months of the Deus Calendar and Their Associated Festivals:

Month of Ice	Start of the New Year
Month of Frost	World Liberation Day (WitchSlayer Celebration)
Month of Song	Spring Equinox
Month of Storms	
Month of Planting	Human+ Festival
Month of Light	Summer Solstice
Month of Soil	
Month of Fire	Summer's End
Month of Falling	Autumn Equinox
Month of Darkness	Hexennacht (Halloween)
Month of Harvest	
Month of Cold	Firefly Hearth Festival
Month of Hearths	Midwinter Celebrations

Timeline

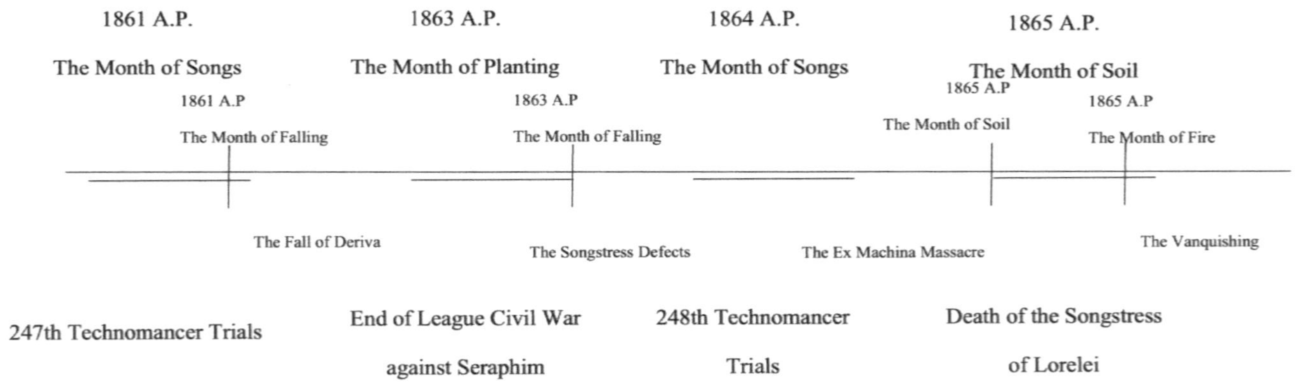

1861 A.P.

The Month of Songs

1861 A.P

The Month of Falling

The Fall of Deriva

247th Technomancer Trials

1863 A.P.

The Month of Planting

1863 A.P

The Month of Falling

The Songstress Defects

End of League Civil War

against Seraphim

1864 A.P.

The Month of Songs

The Ex Machina Massacre

248th Technomancer

Trials

1865 A.P.

The Month of Soil

1865 A.P

The Month of Soil

1865 A.P

The Month of Fire

The Vanquishing

Death of the Songstress

of Lorelei

Timeline

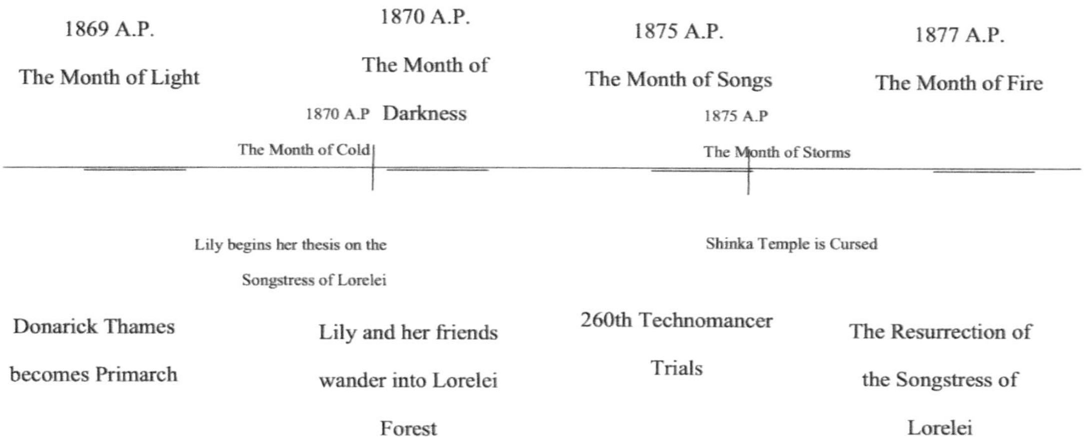

1869 A.P.

The Month of Light

1870 A.P.

The Month of

1870 A.P **Darkness**

The Month of Cold

1875 A.P.

The Month of Songs

1875 A.P

The Month of Storms

1877 A.P.

The Month of Fire

Lily begins her thesis on the
Songstress of Lorelei

Shinka Temple is Cursed

Donarick Thames
becomes Primarch

Lily and her friends
wander into Lorelei
Forest

260th Technomancer
Trials

The Resurrection of
the Songstress of
Lorelei

Glossary of Terms

- Adept – An augmented person equipped with military–grade technology. Certified to hunt and track hexen.
- Aighneas – Largest League country on the west side of the continent. Known for their military, diesel fuel technology, and tank–like machines, Aighneas is similar in culture to the European Union, Canada, and the United States.
- Cyborg – An augmented person possessing a set minimum of technological enhancements, or a human+ possessing enhancements essential to their ability to live (i.e. respiratory life support, mechanical hearts, spinal augmentations to prevent paralysis).
- Deus Ex Machina – Latin – God in the Machine – A storytelling trope in which the author introduces a god or savior–like element to pull their protagonists out of trouble.
- Draugr – An undead creature similar to a revenant or vampire in Scandinavian Folklore. Considered ghosts with corporeal forms, draugr are bloodthirsty and dangerous to humans.
- Fae – Fairy Folk – Magical creatures that pre–date witchcraft in Deus. The Fae generate their own wild magic and live independently of witches (Examples of Fae in Deus: Pixies, Nymphs, Huldra, Mermaids, Trolls).

- Hexen – The Spell Folk – Magic users and creatures reliant or resultant of witchcraft (Examples of Hexen: Witches, Werewolves, Vampyres, Goblins).
- Huldra – A fae, forest guardian originating in Scandinavian Folklore. Huldra are characterized by their cow–like tails, tree–bark backs, and their alluring charms. Said to seduce unsuspecting humans into the woods, sometimes to devour them, other times to reward them, Huldra do not take kindly to trespassers, especially if said trespasser causes damage to their forest.
- Human+ – A person who accepted technology into their existence via a permanent integration. This can be as mediocre an augmentation as a cochlear implant or as extensive as a prosthetic limb or neural net.
- Nøkken – A water spirit originating in Scandinavian Folklore. The Nøkken is said to entertain humans at their shores, enchanting them with a harp or violin. Typically, they are considered benign to humans who are respectful of their waters, but more sinister tales say the Nøkken is an omen of drowning or that the creature is responsible for the drownings themselves.
- Technomancer – A League–certified human+ capable of channelling energy through their technology. Technomancers are specially trained and equipped to hunt and kill dangerous fae, hexen, undead, and other magical creatures. Their augmentations are top–of–the–line and require an immense amount of discipline to maintain and control.
- Witch – A practitioner of witchcraft, the act of molding and utilizing wild magic to effect change in the outer world. Witches in Deus achieve their powers and abilities through a mixture of blood–inheritance and practical study and are considered the most dangerous of beings as the practice of unrestricted magics can lead to psychological breakdown and magic fever.

About the Author

LYRA R. SAENZ IS A WRITER OF SCIENCE fiction/fantasy. A romantic at heart with a love for supernatural horror, she believes that while happy endings don't come easily, they do come, even if it means excising your ex into a glass jar.

Born and raised in South Texas, Lyra is a multicultural, eyeliner–wielding member of the LGBTQ+ community, an animal–lover, and a cynic of all things political. She presently haunts the Houston area with her amazingly supportive partner and her feline–shaped void, Violet. Lyra grew up bouncing between her Chicano and Scandinavian heritages never feeling like she really fit in one world or the other.

Despite growing up on enchiladas and lefsa, she'll never turn down an offering of sushi or pho. And while her friends were getting boyfriends and girlfriends, she was too busy crushing on dreamy anime and manhwa characters to bother with real people. So, with one foot on either side of the border and her head full of East–Asian pop culture, she started creating her own worlds.

A lover of all things witchy, paranormal, and ghostly with a side of Victorian–futurism, cyberpunk, and post-humanism, Lyra imagines worlds where the IT tech is a werewolf, and the coffee machine has a fairy living inside it, but the androids love to take walks down the forest trail and host the occasional bonfire. When she isn't lost somewhere between an inkwell and a notebook, she can be found acting as a throne for the real queen of the household: her cat, and her royal majesty demands snuggles constantly. Or on calmer days, she'll sit and listen to her partner play video games while she unsuccessfully knits and/or binges her latest international tv show.

https://www.bookwitchsaenz.com/

Facebook: BookWitch.Saenz

Twitter: BookWitch_Saenz

Instagram: BookWitch_Saenz

BookWitchSaenz@gmail.com

4 Horsemen Publications
Romance

Ann Shepphird

The War Council

Emily Bunney

All or Nothing
All the Way
All Night Long
All She Needs
Having it All
All at Once
All Together
All for Her

Lynn Chantale

The Baker's Touch
Blind Secrets

Mimi Francis

Private Lives
Second Chances
Run Away Home
The Professor

Fantasy & Paranormal Romance

Beau Lake

The Beast Beside Me
The Beast Within Me
The Beast After Me
The Beast Like Me
An Eye for Emeralds
Swimming in Sapphires
Pining for Pearls

D. Lambert

To Walk into the Sands
Rydan
Northlander
Esparan
King
Traitor
His Last Name

J.M. Paquette

Klauden's Ring
Solyn's Body
The Inbetween
Hannah's Heart
Call Me Forth
Invite Me In

Valerie Willis

Cedric: The Demonic Knight
Romasanta: Father of Werewolves
The Oracle: Keeper of the
Gaea's Gate
Artemis: Eye of Gaea
King Incubus: A New Reign

V.C. Willis

Prince's Priest
Priest's Assassin

Cozy Mysteries

Ann Shepphird

Destination: Maui
Destination: Monterey

Horror, Thriller, & Suspense

Erika Lance

Jimmy
Illusions of Happiness
No Place for Happiness
I Hunt You

Young Adult Fantasy

Blaise Ramsay

Through The Black Mirror
The City of Nightmares
The Astral Tower
The Lost Book of the Old Blood
Shadow of the Dark Witch
Chamber of the Dead God

C.R. Rice

Denial
Anger
Bargaining
Depression
Acceptance
Broken Beginnings:
Story of Thane
Shattered Start: Story of Sera
Sins of The Father: Story of Silas
Honorable Darkness: Story of
Hex and Snip
A Love Lost: Story of Radnar

4HorsemenPublications.com

www.ingramcontent.com/pod-product-compliance
Lightning Source LLC
Chambersburg PA
CBHW050416110726
47899CB00008B/2736